ATET A.D.

FROM A BROKEN BOTTLE TRACES
OF PERFUME STILL EMANATE

ATET A.D.

Nathaniel Mackey

City Lights Books
San Francisco

First Edition
10 9 8 7 6 5 4 3 2 1

www.citylights.com

Cover design by Amy Trachtenberg
Typography by Harvest Graphics

Library of Congress Cataloging-in Publication Data

Mackey, Nathaniel, 1947
   Atet, A.D. / by Nathaniel Mackey
     p. cm. — (From a broken bottle traces of perfume still
emanate ; v. 3)
   ISBN 0-87286-382-4
   1. Jazz musicians — Fiction.   2. Bands (Music) — Fiction
   I. Title: Atet, AD. II Title.
   PS3563.A3166 A94 2001
   813'.54 — dc21   00-065638

CITY LIGHTS BOOKS are edited by Lawrence Ferlinghetti and
Nancy J. Peters and published at the City Lights Bookstore,
261 Columbus Avenue, San Francisco, CA 94133.

Atet A.D. is volume three of *From a Broken Bottle Traces of Perfume Still Emanate*, an ongoing work. Volumes one and two are *Bedouin Hornbook* and *Djbot Baghostus's Run*.

Sections of this book have appeared in *Arras, Avec, Blue Mesa Review, Callaloo, Chain, Chicago Review, The Gig, Hambone, Resonance* and *River City*.

for my sister
Dolores Williams

Dear Angel of Dust,

No doubt by now you've heard the news of Monk's death. What can one say? No doubt there'll now be outpourings of appreciation, much of it from hitherto silent sources, long overdue. It can never amount to more than too little too late. I'm reminded of how I learned of Duke's death in 1974. I was living up north at the time, in Oakland, and was in the habit of listening to the Berkeley Pacifica station, KPFA. Every weekday morning they had a program called "The Morning Concert," two hours of what's commonly called classical. So exclusively was European and Europe-derived "art music" its regimen that when I turned on the program one morning late in May and heard "Black and Tan Fantasy" I knew it could only mean one thing. Well before the announcer came on and said so I knew Duke was dead.

In any event, the way we heard that Monk had died is that Onaje called Lambert the day the news broke to ask if we'd play in a memorial gig at his club that night. It came as no surprise, Monk having been in a coma for more than a week, though that's not to say it had no impact. Still, as I've already said, what can one say? We agreed with no hesitation to take part in the gig, even though Penguin hadn't yet come out of hiding and even though we didn't know when he would. If playing the gig turned out to mean playing without him we were ready to do so.

Penguin's retreat, of course, had given rise to a good deal of comment, concern and speculation among us. Drennette even ventured to wonder out loud one day what kind of trip it was he was on, did he go off that way often and, if so, why do we put up with it. This struck us as a little harsh and to me at least it suggested she had a deeper emotional investment in Penguin's doings than she let on. Aunt Nancy wasted no time speaking up. She called Penguin's "trip" an "occupational hazard," repeating Baraka's line that music makes you think of a lot of weird things and that it can even make you become one of them. Clearly, she suggested, Penguin had.

I spoke up as well. Penguin's retreat, I said, struck me as related to something he once told me about Monk. I recounted his telling me of Monk getting into moods in which he'd answer the phone by grumbling, "Monk's not here," then hang up. Penguin's own telephonically announced retreat, I suggested, amounted to a kind of couvade. It was a case of sympathetic ordeal, him turning away from the world in solidarity with Monk. How it came to me to say this I can't entirely say. It simply popped into my head as I spoke. I can, however, say that I deliberately downplayed Penguin's attraction to Drennette, thinking it might be the source of her annoyance. I steered clear of his would-be rap, the aborted recitation I knew was at the root of his retreat. This doesn't, however, explain the particulars which popped into my head to take its place. Nor does it explain why I persisted along these lines even after I saw that my not mentioning his attraction to her seemed to increase instead of lessen Drennette's annoyance. I'm tempted to say that I could feel Penguin feeding me my lines, just as with "E Po Pen," but it wouldn't be true. All I felt was the pull and the appeal of the Monk angle, the fact that it so perfectly fit. (Indeed, so much so that I wondered, even as I spoke, had I gotten things wrong in "E Po Pen," thought Mingus when I should've thought Monk.)

The impromptu connection I drew between Penguin's retreat and Monk's coma seemed to be borne out by what subsequently occurred, the fact that Penguin chose to make his return at the memorial gig. We had no way, as I've already said, of knowing whether he would emerge in time for the gig. Lambert called and left a message on his machine, giving him the details, but by that night, not having heard from him, we accepted having to play without him.

A good-sized crowd showed up at Onaje's. A small place, it was pretty much packed. Considering the short notice, word had gotten around pretty well. Besides us, a number of other bands from around town took part. We each played what was supposed to be a thirty-minute set, though in most cases it turned out more like forty-five. Our set came fairly late, as we were the fifth group to play. We followed a trio led by Badi Taqsim, a pianist who's been turning a lot of heads lately. He mainly plays other people's compositions, among them a good number of standards, but the touch he puts on them is all his own. They finished up their set with a couple of pieces which really tore the place up—Monk's "Pannonica," followed by a John Lewis piece hardly anyone ever does, "Natural Affection." A wistful strain had run thru the set, held in check or bitten back, however, by Monk's ironic pluck and puckish good humor (all the pieces they played, save the last one, were Monk pieces). "Pannonica" took the standoff between wistful plaint and ironic pluck to an almost unbearable pitch before the Lewis piece exacted a surprising denouement. How piano, bass and drums could effect a breathy timbral suspension worthy of Charlie Rouse himself I'll never know, but they somehow did on the former. All the built-up tension, the austere articulacy and the sense of incomplete release "Natural Affection" then took into another domain. The bossa nova beat, coming after the solemnity of the piece's opening chords, took most of the audience by surprise, introducing an abrupt, dilated liquidity, an agile dilation finessed on several fronts at once. Wistfulness turned into *saudade*.

As I stood there listening I couldn't help remembering that the quality the Brazilians call *saudade* goes back to the home-sickness the slaves felt for Africa. A Brazilian friend of mine told me this a few years back and it struck me that Badi must have known it as well, so apt was the evocation of "going home" to the occasion. What got to me was what almost always does with bossa nova, the mix of compliance, complication and complaint it brings off. The piece, that is, was one in which longing, heavily tinged with regret, became complicit with a no-regrets furtherance of itself or beyond itself, a self-possessed rhythmic advance which, when it was on, ran the line between "of" and "beyond."

But I've gotten caught up with something I really didn't mean to go on about so long. Suffice it to say that we were there, Badi's trio reminded us, to see Monk home, that their reading of the piece more than rose to the occasion, so gently thrusted was its mating of tendency with touch, that they more than made it live up to its title. Which is also to say that they put us in just the right mood, just the right frame of mind. They put us in touch with a well of affection we repeatedly had recourse to throughout our set (though "put us in touch" wasn't so much what it was as that they variously apprised us we already were).

Penguin chose to show up at the gig, as I've already said, but we were well into our set by the time he did. We had just finished "Reflections," our rendition of which, though I hate to brag, was a killer. With Aunt Nancy on violin and Djamilaa doubling on harmonium and bandoneon, we gave it an Indo-Argentine reading which, by way of tempo changes here and there, insisted on links between tango and Baul. Lambert and I both played tenor, both of us heavily indebted to Sonny Rollins's Blue Note recording of the piece, most notably the sense of alarm he gets from the leap to high D in the fifth bar.

We gave it that same quantum sense of duress but added a touch of our own, pulling back as if to declare the alarm false. If you can imagine the acoustical equivalent of a fade-away jumpshot you've got a good idea of the approach we took. Aunt Nancy complicated the figure once or twice with a sirenlike shooting-pain bowswipe recalling Piazzolla's violinist Fernando Paz. Anyway, it all added up to murder—so much so Onaje joked with us later he'd considered calling the coroner's office. Things got even more lethal with our next and, as it turned out, final number, "In Walked Bud." I went over to alto, Djamilaa switched to piano and Aunt Nancy went from violin to bass. Djamilaa played the first eight bars unaccompanied, the rest of us joining in on the first repeat. It was at the beginning of the second repeat that we heard an oboe join in from near the club's entrance, perfectly in tune and right on the beat. We looked out over the heads of the audience, all of whom had turned around to see who the oboist was, and there was Penguin playing away while slowly making his way toward the stage. We went into yet another repeat and still another and, before it was over, several more—an impromptu vamp-till-ready as we waited for Penguin to reach the stage.

Once Penguin was onstage one couldn't help noticing how disheveled he was. He hadn't shaved, his hair hadn't been combed and his clothes looked as if he'd slept in them. What's more, he appeared to have slept outdoors. Twigs, bits of dry grass and even leaves clung to his clothes and to his hair. (We later learned he'd spent the time he'd been away camping out near the Hollywood Reservoir.) One also couldn't help noticing how different he sounded, the expansive, magisterial sound he got from the horn, a voluminous thrust and dimensionality which was all the more pronounced now that he blew into a mike. This was a bigger, rounder, more hollowed-out, holier sound than he'd ever gotten, a sound he sought to

after the other he and I should do so at the same time, trade choruses and so forth, make it a dialogue, a duet. This I agreed to. When Aunt Nancy finished her solo the two of us took up what turned out to be an extended, increasingly contentious conversation. Penguin, I quickly found out, took exception to "E Po Pen," felt it trivialized his retreat. It made too much of his aborted rap to Drennette, too much of the torch it alleged he carried for Djeannine. This he insisted by way of a bold, falsetto run which embraced "high would" in order to complain of my "low blow." He ended the run by quoting the stuttering, low-register croak Wayne Shorter gets into towards the end of his solo on "Fee-Fi-Fo-Fum," one of the pieces on the *Speak No Evil* album, the point of neither title missing its mark. With that we were off on what ended up being duet, duel and dozens rolled into one. Though a bit surprised at first, Aunt Nancy, Drennette and Djamilaa egged us on, as tight and on-top-of-it a rhythm section as one could want, and Lambert threw in an exhortative two or three notes every now and then. It was somewhat like Freddie Hubbard and Lee Morgan's exchanges on *The Night of the Cookers*, Hawkins and Rollins's on *Sonny Meets Hawk*, Mingus and Dolphy's on "What Love" or "So Long Eric." What it came down to was an old-time cuttin' session.

I won't attempt to give you a detailed account. Let me let it go at saying that I held my ground as best I could, arguing that "E Po Pen" struck me as being dictated to me by him (to which he replied I was blaming the victim), that, in any case, a little humor never hurt anyone (to which he replied we'd see who'd laugh last), that, even so, it was his Djeannine dream and only his which had the broken-tooth ending (to which he replied so what), and so forth. It was some of the hottest, heaviest going I've ever taken part in. We worked what seemed like a million variations on "In Walked Bud" and by the end had come up with a new tune that you'll find on the tape I've enclosed. Penguin and I recorded it yesterday, just the two of us, unaccompanied. We set out to recapture what we did at Onaje's and, allowing for the inevitable variances, we succeeded. We call the piece "In Walked Pen."

The thing worth pointing out about both the tape and our duel/duet at Onaje's is that Penguin ultimately prevailed by turning my "low blow" against me. Somehow during his retreat he managed to add a full octave to the bottom end of the oboe's range. Towards the end of our duel/duet he lured me into what amounted to a limbo match, a test of who could go lower. (It was this match, in fact, which brought both our duel/duet and the piece to a conclusion. It also, that night at Onaje's, ended our set, "In Walked Bud" having gone on longer than we'd planned as a result of Penguin showing up.) The alto being pitched over half an octave lower than the oboe, I figured I had it made. He surprised me and everyone else, though, by working his way down past the horn's low B-flat to an even lower B-flat, almost half an octave lower than mine. As he did so I could've sworn I heard the rafters rattle and felt the floor shake. I made the futile gesture of putting my knee in the bell of my horn to play A, though I knew that didn't even come close to making up the difference. Penguin had beat me at what he insisted was my own game, deftly augmenting "high would" with "low would," a stunning move to which my A was a lame comeback, next to none at all. Had it been knives rather than horns we battled with I'd have bled to death.

As ever,

N.

Dear Angel of Dust,

Thanks for writing back so soon. What a surprise to receive your "liner notes" to "In Walked Pen." I appreciate your once again encouraging us to put out a record, even more your willingness to write the notes for it. The idea of a "test run" is a good one and I'm glad you thought of it, glad you acted on it as well. I've read your "run" a couple of times and I'm very excited. I particularly like the use you make of narration. Yes, every tune does tell a story. The coy, contingent yarn you spin teases out—instructively so—"In Walked Pen's" oblique, centrifugal drift. I also like the length you give it. Do you remember those Limelight albums in the sixties, the ones that opened up sort of like a book and had several pages of liner notes? That's the kind of thing I'd want done with what you've written.

There's one thing, though, I have problems with: the way you belabor the relationship of Penguin's boastful, magisterial sound to rap music. It's not that your play on his would-be rap to Drennette is lost on me, nor that rap isn't the latest in a long tradition of black (male mostly) self-praise and contestual display, a tradition of which our duel/duet is obviously a part. No, it's more a matter of scale and perspective. I wouldn't want anyone to get the idea we were pandering to fashion, putting undue emphasis on something simply because it's in. I'd feel more at ease with your notes if you gave more attention to the wider matrix rap's a part of, were you to drop a few of the rap references for some mention of, say, Memphis Slim's "Sweet Root Man," Bo Diddley's "Who Do You Love," Dexter Gordon's "Soy Califa" (or, for that matter, Pete "El Conde" Rodriguez's "Soy La Ley"), John Lee Hooker's "I'm Bad Like Jesse James," Lord Invader's "Me

One Alone" or any number of others too numerous to list. There's nothing new about swagger.

What *is* new is that since I last wrote there's begun to be talk about changing the name of the band. It was Drennette who brought it up. She complained at rehearsal the other day that "Mystic Horn Society" privileges the horns, emphasizes them at the other instruments' expense. She went on to say that since our sound wouldn't be what it is were *any* of the instruments missing she saw no reason to single out the horns as in some way worthy of special notice. It was a point none of us could disagree with. Aunt Nancy was quick to chime in that not only was Drennette right but that the problem went farther, that the name smacks of male privilege, given that the horns are played primarily by the men in the group. "To say nothing," she capped it off by saying, "of the phallic associations horns have."

This last remark had a funny effect on me. I had no problem with Drennette's complaint, nor with Aunt Nancy's addendum apropos male privilege. Something inside me, however, instinctively objected to the "phallic associations" bit, the easy, one-sided equation it rested on, the reductiveness of it. The phrase triggered — antithetically triggered — the recollection of a dream I hadn't thought about in years. Almost before I knew it I found myself speaking up to say that while I agreed with almost everything that had been said I thought the phallic bit was going too far. I then proceeded to recount, as a counter example, the dream which had just come back to me again, a dream I'd had when I was about eight, the circumstances surrounding which I recounted as well. I explained that as a kid I was a big fan of rock and roll — Little Richard, Chuck Berry, Bill Haley and the like — and that I was also under the influence of the church, that my mother, at my grandmother's insistence, had started me going to Sunday School when I was five. I explained that I thought about Judgment Day a lot and that having heard that to listen to rock and roll was a sin had me worried. I found it hard to believe it was and different people gave different opinions, but, I explained further, I worried about it anyway. I then recounted how one night I decided to settle the question, how when I said my prayers that night I asked God to send me a sign: to make me dream of pirates if it was true that listening to rock and roll was a sin, to make me dream of cowboys if it wasn't. I went on to how it ended up I dreamt about neither pirates nor cowboys that night but dreamt instead I was in a dark room in which I heard a sinuous, arresting piece of music played on what sounded like a cross between a trumpet and a bassoon; how it went on that way for a while, me standing in the dark, unable to see anything, caught up in the music; how finally a spotlight came on and illumined a figure quite some distance away from me and how with that it became clear that this figure was where the music was coming from; how I knew now I was in a large auditorium and began walking toward the spotlighted figure; how as I got closer I could tell the figure was a woman and, closer yet, that she had no clothes on and that the music was as much a scent as it was a sound, a synaesthetic mix (part music, part musk), a penetrating mist of sound which was earthy, ethereal, refined and funky, all at the same time; how as I got even closer I could tell the music emanated from a horn between the spotlighted woman's thighs, a cornucopic horn without the grapes and so forth, though I couldn't make out whether it was a part of her body or simply held in place by pressure put on it by her legs; how when I reached the stage and finally stood in front of her I couldn't resist sticking my nose up over the lip of the horn to "smell" the music better; how when I did my eyes crossed and rolled around before closing and my head shot back in slow motion as I went into a swoon.

Dear Angel of Dust,

I found myself going back to your "liner notes" again and again over the past few days. The ipseic surmise they engage the music with kept calling me back—that along with a wish to have my own way with what you'd written, a wish I couldn't quite shake even though I told myself I should. It's not so much that I had quarrels with your take on the piece as that the more I read your notes the more it seemed I stood on revisionary ground, so exponential the seismic suzerainty ipseity served. Sesame squared I'm tempted to call it, Earth of sesame to the second power, ground grown rich with susurrant seed, an open aliquance insisting on emendation. (One of Cecil Taylor's titles, "Chorus of Seed," comes to mind.) Seismic seed not only fed me but, as if I were a muscle, flexed me. I found myself changing words here and there, making notes in the margins, putting my own stylistic spin on this, that and the other. That spin bore an antithetical bent, the ongoing gist or gestation of an *opera contra naturam*. Your notes were clearly lecture/libretto material. The results you'll find enclosed.

As you can see, the changes are not that radical. I followed your lead at all points. Your notes ended up, it seems to me, not so much rewritten as differently pitched. Seismic seed's pneumatic sprout, however much it recast or reconceived your tack, for the most part reconfirmed it.

Anyway, let me know what you think.

Yours,

N.

IN WALKED PEN

or, The Creaking of the Word: After-the-Fact Lecture/Libretto (A.D. Version)

Penguin's return coincided with the news of Monk's death. Newly descended from an ancient line of authority figures, he came back having crowned himself King Pen. Some, he knew, would think of King Oliver, King Pleasure, King Curtis, Nat King Cole. Duke, Prez, Count, Prince Lasha and others would also come to mind. It went, in fact, much farther back than any of them, farther back than he himself had initially suspected. It went farther back than the 'Lection Day fifes and drums he'd heard the moment the crown touched his head, farther back than the Pinkster eelpot he'd heard not more than a split-second after that.

King Pen had come into antiphonal play with "monastic flight," Penguin's loose, euphemistic term for Monk's death. A funereal wedding of church and state, nominal kingship heralded the end of charismatic retreat. The quality Lambert once referred to as Monk's "renunciative harmonics" had long struck a mendicant chord deep within. Even so, Penguin seized upon the occasion of "monastic flight" (a further phase of the mock-awkward mantle, the gnostic shrug Monk so regally wore) to inaugurate a new recourse to power, a return to the world.

"I went off," Penguin announced on his return, "to prepare a place. The alternate authority of would-be kings no longer sufficed. Gassire's lute-song notwithstanding, I went after an order of metathetic spin which would, pardon the expression, cash in on a eurhythmic aplomb typically consecrated to forfeiture, debility, loss." He stopped, feeling he sounded too rhetorical. N. had already heard it all anyway.

Penguin had gone off to Wouldly Ridge but he'd kept N. abreast of his thoughts off and on, getting in touch by telepathic dispatch when some such incident of note as his coronation came up. N. too had heard the fifes and drums and the Pinkster eelpot the moment the crown touched Penguin's head. They'd both also heard a voice — a faint, faraway voice which asked, "Who are our true rulers?" Possessed of a strong nineteenth-century accent, the voice, barely pausing a beat, went on to answer, "The Negro poets, to be sure. Do they not set the fashion, and give laws to the public taste? Let one of them, in the swamps of Carolina, compose a new song, and it no sooner reaches the ear of a white amateur, than it is written down, amended (that is, almost spoilt), printed, and then put upon a course of rapid dissemination, to cease only with the utmost bounds of Anglo-Saxondom, perhaps with the world. Meanwhile, the poor author digs away with his hoe, utterly ignorant of his greatness." That they'd both heard it had to do with the odd bond Penguin's retreat had brought to the surface, the otherwise Atlantislike relational "glue" which took the place of place. It was as if the "place" he'd gone off to prepare was not so much a place as a certain rapport, a "place" neither wholly here nor wholly there. It was a "place" which was more than one place at once, a utopic ubiquity which, though always there, was never all there.

Nonetheless, Penguin's hideaway had indeed been a place. Tucked away in a wooded area near the Hollywood Reservoir, Wouldly Ridge overlooked the L.A. Basin. It was there Penguin had pitched his tent after taking a run around the reservoir. Indian vision quest and early American camp meeting rolled into one, his retreat had begun with an unbased ring shout, the atavistic shuffle he took his jog around the reservoir to be.

Before going off Penguin had suffered a romantic setback. This was widely known to be the reason he went off. Going into hiding near the reservoir was an attempt to get back in touch with something he feared had begun to get away. His womanly thought-soul he called it, adopting the Dogon idea of a female intelligent kikínu held in reserve in the family pool —an idea N. had turned him on to some time ago. Perhaps it was this which had made for the brotherly rapport which telepathically kept the two of them in touch.

"'Cash in,'" Penguin resumed after a pause, "isn't quite the right way to put it." He paused again. His mouth was dry. He was no longer sure he had N.'s attention. Afraid he'd see that he didn't, he looked away, out the living room window, deliberately avoiding eye contact.

As the two of them sat there in N.'s living room the odd, psychosomatic thirst from which he'd suffered while on Wouldly Ridge again, for a moment, parched his mouth and throat. It had been a thirst he couldn't shake no matter how much he drank, a thirst made all the more intransigent, it seemed, by the nearness of the reservoir. It had been as if water was there in too much abundance, as if the thought of so much held in reserve refuted satiety. If, as he'd once read, thirst proves water's existence, wasn't the converse also true? The whole time on Wouldly Ridge he'd felt like a dying man on a desert, his thirst seeming at times, deliriously, like a thirst for diminution, a wish that the reservoir were smaller, the watery, womanly thought-soul he sought to replenish notwithstanding. "A spoonful," he'd found himself muttering, "just a spoonful." "Spoonful" had become a kind of mantra he often resorted to over the course of his retreat. "Spoonful, spoonful," he'd intone from time to time, seeking to soothe (and to some degree succeeding) his parched mouth and throat's insatiate "fling" with proximate water.

N. looked at Penguin, who continued gazing out the window. He wondered what had made him fall silent. No longer telepathically in touch, he had no way of knowing that Penguin's thoughts were on Wouldly Ridge, that he sat absorbed in recollecting the spill he'd suffered three days into his retreat. Even so, he himself felt a slight centrifugal rush as a somewhat stronger centrifugal rush took hold of Penguin, an ultimately phantom centrifugal sense of being swirled or swung or, "ec-" to "centric" water, flung. This was the sense Penguin had had during his run around the reservoir on day three of his retreat—not so much a mere sense, though, as an outright force causing his legs to cross and him to go tumbling to the ground.

"At first I felt it had to be that I was being punished," Penguin muttered, more to himself than to N. but breaking the silence nonetheless. He continued to not make eye contact, gazing out the window. "My centrifugal fling with womanly water had led to a fall. An ever so faint atavistic voice pointed out that my legs had crossed and for a moment I'd been dancing. My head hit the ground and I saw the Big Dipper, the 'drinking gourd' the same voice had said I should follow. It seemed to rebuke the diminution I sought, cosmically magnify the mantric spoonful I'd invoked. Oddly enough, it was then, I think, that my accession to the throne began, adumbrated by the 'starry crown,' to use the voice's expression, I saw swirling right above my head. There was something baptismal about the astral splash my spill brought me abreast of. Yes, my head hit the ground and I saw stars. This was the wet celestial seed of which King Pen appears to've been born."

N. wasn't sure he got Penguin's drift but he went on listening without interrupting. Penguin had sent no telepathic dispatch on this matter. This was the first he'd heard of the spill. It gave him a lot to think about and he was having a hard time keeping up. Did Penguin mean to suggest, he wondered,

that he himself (that is, Penguin) had assumed the role of
womanly water? Did he mean to say that he'd been dipped
into, that the "starry crown," the magnified spoonful, capped
an interior, "southern" sky? The long journey from humble
gourd to coronal spoonful he could follow, though he'd have
wanted it to be a northward one. Was it, after all, merely sub-
limation, he wondered, couvade?

Drennette, N. remembered, had suffered a spill she cred-
ited with revelatory impact, an epiphanous bicycle accident
she said had turned her sense of things around. Did Penguin
seek to spark some sort of parallel with her by claiming to
have similarly suffered a revelatory spill? Did he mean to
show that he too could invoke a blow to the head, that the ini-
tiatic tie between spill and spirit was an experiential truth to
which he too was now privy? If so, in what spirit did he seek
to do so? Was it rapport or was it one-up-manship he sought?
Did he mean to install himself as King to Drennette's Queen
or was he claiming a throne all to himself? Why had he so far
made no mention of her? These were the questions N. sat
asking himself while Penguin made such pronouncements as
"I gave birth to myself on Wouldly Ridge," "King Pen is for
real and it's him I really am," "Monk died so King Pen could
be born."

After a while N. could sit quietly no longer. "What about
Drennette?" he interrupted to ask.

Penguin stopped talking but went on gazing out the win-
dow. He himself realized he'd suffered multiple blows. The
blow to his head when he fell while jogging had been followed
the next day by the news of Monk's death. The problematic
turn his interest in Drennette had taken, he had to admit, was
the blow to which those two were like aftershocks. The
looped allusion to womanly water to which his run around the
reservoir amounted he continued to conceive as a ring shout

— unbased because of Drennette's anti-antiphonal silence. Her non-response had sent him off in search of inner resources, the atavistic, "southern" chorus whose antiphonal support placed him on the throne. He caught the point of N.'s question at once and wanted to answer that the throne was solely the King's, that it rested on antiphonal authority which wasn't hers, that Drennette could in no way be said to be his Queen. On the other hand, he quickly admitted to himself, Drennette's non-response had mothered his need to give birth to King Pen, his need to break womanly water to become his own unmatched body of water — to *thirst*, outward water notwithstanding. "Yes," he said, turning at last to look at N., "for a time the throne I sought was the oceanic sway of Drennette's hips. I'm way beyond that now. King Pen sits on his own." It was a surprising way to put it, surprising even to himself, and he paused to reflect a moment before going on. "The fifes and drums and the Pinkster eelpot I heard made it clear I'd made it north, that no matter how compensatory it appeared it was no mirage. No, this was no 'southern' sky lit by an illusory Dipper, no wishful pursuit of illusory depth, no illusory spoonful's putative plunge. No, this was true north."

N. felt he'd been caught out. He himself had heard the fifes and drums and the Pinkster eelpot, a fact which didn't leave much room for the kinds of questions he'd been entertaining. The slight centrifugal rush he'd felt should also have taught him something. What was at stake was the nature of true rule, the circumambular cast of an antiphonal north natively known to be true, quixotic needle notwithstanding. Penguin had apparently picked up on this, apparently read his thoughts or in some other way known that "What about Drennette?" was a loaded question. His powers were not to be dismissed or taken lightly. King Pen had to be reckoned with.

All of this N. already knew. Penguin did nothing more than make him admit it. Native knowledge went a long way to "explain" circumambular north but in the end had not really gone anywhere. What had gone was explanation itself, the tangential demand put on perimetric spill by centric water.

For a short while they sat silently looking at one another. Penguin then turned his head and went back to gazing out the window, whereupon N. once more felt a slight centrifugal rush. The inexplicable sense of having been flung caused a shiver to run up his back, a sharp, anti-explanatory twinge which made him sit up straight. "Explanation," he found himself saying, "is the pail of water we used to dance with atop our heads in slavery times. Would you agree that post-explanatory spillage's 'Hush now, don't' takes the cake nowadays?"

Penguin turned and looked at N. again, a look on his face which seemed to ask what was going on. N.'s tangential comment had touched on the limits of explanatory truth, the perimetric defects of circumambular persuasion, circular trope and treadmill rolled into one. Even so, N. again found himself tempted. An explanatory model proposed itself in which the would-be bond between phallic plunge and philosophic spoonful surfaced again. Before he could stop himself he gave in to it, taking advantage of Penguin's non-response to insist, "You've still got a chance with Drennette if you'll only come down from Would-Be Ridge."

No sooner had N. said this than they both felt a further centrifugal rush, an oblique furtherance of an emergent prospect or principle whose outline remained obscure. The lateral drift accelerated by N.'s pointed play on "Wouldly" was not without a vertical aspect, a sense of tilt, disorientation or erosion which made it feel as though as they slid they lost elevation as well. "Would-Be Ridge's" intimation of unreliable support, much to N.'s own chagrin, fostered a sense that the

floor sank as they slid across it. He himself couldn't shake the
feeling that he slid upon a precipitous ledge, inexplicably
dependent upon a hypothetic surface which might not have
been there. Thus it was that epithetic "Would-Be"
boomeranged against him. He found he'd cast a more inclu-
sive net than he'd intended. Not only had he reversed his ear-
lier position regarding Drennette (encouraging Penguin to
pursue her whereas before he'd urged him to cool it), he'd
also cast aspersions on Wouldly Ridge. Neither of these had
he intended to do. It was this, the irrelevance of intention,
which undermined his living room floor, made it more and
more hypothetic. Hypothetic floor, moreover, might as well
have been epithetic Ridge — a reversal which was by no
means lost on him.

Penguin, on the other hand, endured the further centrifu-
gal rush and the sense of tilt with the firm conviction that they
were evidence of King Pen's power. Tangential drift and the
loss of elevation paradoxically bolstered the throne on which
he sat. Tilt and slide recalled the oceanic sway he'd spoken of
in regard to Drennette's hips, an ironic accession to the
"throne" he'd earlier insisted he'd gone beyond. With this he
rubbed N.'s innuendo in his face, tilt and slide taking less time
than the blinking of an eye, at the end of which he sat grin-
ning with satisfaction. "I didn't come here to be insulted," he
told N. He'd made it clear that King Pen didn't play.

N. understood he'd been put in his place. The pail of water
crowning the slave's head, he reflected, might as well have
been a dunce's cap. Penguin had answered with an antiphonal
spoonful, an ever so slight bit of spillage he'd endowed with
the movement of a wave about to break. Crest, crown and
womanly rump rolled into one, the tilting, sliding sense of a
"spilling" floor had brought N. up short. That this had
occurred at all would've been wonder enough. That it was

done with a mere spoonful of water — spilled water — humbled him all the more.

Having made it clear that King Pen didn't play, Penguin now went on to insist that "What about Monk?" was much more to the point. "Monastic flight," he said, "brought home to me the fact that in retreating to Wouldly Ridge I was looking for a meeting of would-be king with worldly king, the fact that wouldly reign sought to reconcile the two. Monkish, renunciative accent unquenchably thirsted after wouldly rule. That this was the case was all the more obvious now that Monk was gone. When I heard the news I couldn't help thinking of 'New Monastery,' Andrew's piece. The title of the album it's on, *Point of Departure*, ratified my sense of tangential vocation. Call it the rendezvous of *tendency* with *point*, or, better yet, say that the prospect of punctual access *lifted*, possessed of a centrifugal 'high.'"

Penguin fell silent, his head slightly tilted like a bird's. The implications of lifted access caused him to pause and reflect a while. Tendency and point's conjunctive capture, their joint possession by centrifugal "high," felt as if point no longer yielded to explanatory pressure.

N. studied the look on Penguin's face while giving some thought to what he'd said. It was an odd, not entirely convincing take, he thought, having more to do with Monk's name than with the music or the man. Still, the Andrew Hill piece to which Penguin had referred happened to be one of his favorites. The mix of watery verticality and angular surge it pulled off had taken hold of him what seemed like ages ago. The mere mention of it now filled his head with the synaesthetic images of staggered ignition which had filled it the first time he heard the piece — subaquatic fountains and jets, underwater fireworks giving Penguin's pursuit of womanly thought-soul all the more oomph. Even so, N. continued to apply a grain of salt to Penguin's take on Monk's death, a take he increasingly felt to be offbase — deliberately so, therapeutically so perhaps, but bordering on disrespect all the same. He had a hard time not meeting disrespect with disrespect, a hard time refraining from asking, "What about Djeannine? What about lilac time?"

Repressing the question hurt the tip of his tongue. It was a question alluding to a song which had recently come to his attention, a song Gene Austin recorded in the twenties, "Jeannine, I Dream of Lilac Time." That the song had been featured in a movie, *Lilac Time*, a movie starring Colleen Moore and Gary Cooper, made the question all the more sarcastic. Behind its dig lay the lines "Jeannine, my queen of lilac time, / When I return, I'll make you mine." Penguin's return, the question implied, was mere fantasy resolution, King Pen's throne a mere would-be seat beside his dream-queen Djeannine.

It was an allusion, however, whose bite would've been lost on Penguin. N. himself had only recently learned of the song, having happened upon Austin's recording on an album he found in a used record store. He had no reason to believe Penguin had ever heard of it. The question was thus one whose dig he'd have to explain — all the more reason, he admitted, not to ask it. Even so, it took an immense effort to hold it back, so immense he literally bit his tongue, applied a steady, clamplike pressure with his teeth. As he did so he couldn't help wondering was reverse bite, boomeranging bite, yet another demonstration of King Pen's power.

N.'s nose now began to twitch. The smell of lilacs wafted in from some abrupt, immediately suspect source he thought of turning his head to try to catch offguard — a thought it took no more than a moment to reject. Years ago he'd read liner notes on an Eric Dolphy album, notes which spoke of

Dolphy's "impatience," his wish to "sneak" past limits. "He implies beyond the horn," the notes had asserted. "He tries to sneak through its limitations at some swift, flat angle." The passage had stayed with him, stuck in his mind, more or less verbatim. It was exactly that "swift, flat angle" from which he now felt himself addressed, an obtuse, tangential angle thru which the lilac scent made its way. The resistance of any such angle to attribution argued against turning his head. He knew too well it would've done no good.

The clamplike pressure of his teeth on his tongue and the angular advent of lilac scent made for a synaesthetic wad of apprehension to which the eelpot's return was now added. The sound of it came in loud and clear, entering at exactly the same "swift, flat angle" the smell of lilacs took. Smell, touch and hearing were rolled into one by the lilac vibe, an unsettling mix which made it evident that Penguin had not only read his thoughts but succeeded in turning them against him again. The eelpot completed the combination which took him out, an epiphanous "click" not unlike sesame access except that it was clamp-lilac-eelpot access instead.

Yes, he now knew for sure, reverse bite, boomeranging bite, was another demonstration of King Pen's power. A split-second before he passed out he glimpsed a spoon spinning slowly like the blade of a fan just above Penguin's head, a suspended "crown" which, hovering halolike, confirmed the now uncontested majesty of King Pen.

Dear Angel of Dust,

What I called clamp-lilac-eelpot access in my lecture/
libretto has turned a new page in the band's book. We've all
fallen in with a flow we always knew was there, though not as
viscerally as we know it now. We've again been apprised of an
echoic whir, warned against pre-emptive equivalence. The
aliquant register unveiled by Penguin's "low would" run, the
kingly descent which put him on his "throne," conferred a
false-fingered, winged as well as winded benediction on one
and all—a dry, self-appointing anointment both in and out of
keeping with a prosaic age. "Low would" run spoke of blown
resources, a desultory, deciduous calculus of last resort.
Winded, wing-and-a-prayer benediction blew thru from the
lips of a desiderative muse.

This has all become increasingly evident as the days have
gone by since Penguin's return. What I thought at first was a
local hit—what in fact was at first a local hit—has turned out
to be a sustained buzz, a namesake bud which eventually
bloomed. Infectious wind and incongruous wing rolled into
one, it carried a spark which didn't stop with me and Penguin
but went on to light up Aunt Nancy, Djamilaa, Lambert and
Drennette as well. That it took a while to spread takes noth-
ing away from it. It makes it all the more formidable in fact.
Part spore, part resuscitated fossil, it's for real. Something
new seems to be afoot.

Djamilaa and I were talking about this last night. She
spoke of Penguin's epiphany as the realization that "would"
works both ways. He came to see, she said, that he'd set him-
self up to be let down, that the would-be high he projected
held hands with would-be low, that Drennette, just like every-

one else, was as much the one as she was the other. His "low would" run, she went on, sought to announce this realization triumphantly, to proclaim it as an edict he was the author of. That the bottom falls out to reveal another bottom was clearly the point of the wouldly octave he blew. Wouldly reign, she elaborated, the recognition of "would's" two-way cut, gave welcome relief to ostensible bottom, see-thru bottom. It was here that she got to the part that spoke to me most. To've been taken up, she said, by "low would" run, as we clearly have, is to be seated in a glass-bottom boat.

It was this I was thinking about today at rehearsal when I suggested we give "Sun Ship" a try. I've long been drawn to the percussive, sculptor's approach Trane takes to its iterative head (as though he chipped or hammered away at stone), the rhythmic seizure which translates shock into shapeliness. I knew it would put the visceral flow we've fallen in with to a test, but something told me it was a test we could pass. In any case, the prospect of a glass-bottom ride (wouldly ride) in the company of no less than the Sun was one I couldn't see passing up.

It turned out to be all I'd expected, even more — a ride unlike any we'd ever known. To say that *lapse* was the element we moved in begins to give some sense of what it was like, though to say that a navigable inordinacy opened up begins to as well. A condition of catch-up, that is, with all the turbulence and winded urgency thus implied (wouldly weather), came into complicated play with glass-bottom repose. Iterative head, it seemed, charted a zigzag, serrate course. It was as if we sought to stitch two pieces of cloth together, to close the rift between Wouldly River's two banks, to bite thru the element we rode even though to do so proposed its undoing. It was this bite which brought clamp into the picture, a clenched, mandibular coefficient which, even so, left one's embouchure as open as one could want. One sang thru one's teeth as lilacs bloomed on both banks. Eels wiggled by below.

Mandibular clench was both a courtesy and a caution. I looked around and saw that everyone's jaws were a little tight. It was as if we bit back or fought back further expression even as we gave the piece all the expressive propulsion we could. We each, it seemed, had clenching recourse to the old blues line, "Don't start me talkin'"—a disingenuous disclaimer animating the reservoir it sought to conserve. Consumption and conservation locked hands. Glass-bottom advance insisted on the ultimacy of see-thru bottom, albeit "see-thru" declared ultimacy void.

Reservoir notwithstanding, it was the flow clamp-lilac-eelpot calibrated which was most worth noting. We all hunched forward—a flow-thru posture—as we played. I was relieved, as I looked around, to see it wasn't just me. Djamilaa hunched forward over the piano, as did Drennette over the drumset, Aunt Nancy over the bass, Penguin and Lambert, just like me, over their tenors. The band roared like a three-horned beast. The three tenors played the head in unison, then improvised all at the same time (shades of Trane, Pharoah and Donald Garrett on the *Live in Seattle* date), a tricorn crown to which Penguin alluded at one point with a quote from Rahsaan's "We Free Kings." The relationship of crown to head, as was only to be expected of wouldly reign, grew faint, far-fetched at times—the ravings of thwarted royalty, would-be kings. Wouldly roar's tricorn crown went Alexander the Great, the Two-Horned, one better.

Kings in Exile, a band in Dallas whose record *Music from Ancient Texts* we've been listening to of late, was clearly in the backs of our minds—not so much their music as the outcast kingship their name evokes. This went well with the Nilotic rush the rhythm section laid down, the magic, magisterial car-

peacefully and kindly, but after a few years he's ruling with such cruelty the people plot to get rid of him. The method they decide on is poison. They put a poison made from powdered Tosaut rock on his chest one night while he's asleep. He wakes up to feel a sickness in his limbs and at length dies.

I've been reading *The Black Jacobins*, C. L. R. James's book on Toussaint L'Ouverture and the Haitian Revolution, and I couldn't help thinking of the use of poison he writes about early on, the fact that the slaves resorted to it so often. (The notorious Mackandal, he says, built up his organization for six years, he and his followers poisoning both whites and disobedient members of their own band. They had a plan to launch an uprising by poisoning the water of every house in the capital.) I also couldn't help recalling that the most intractable slaves were the so-called saltwater Negroes, those who'd made the Middle Passage. The title "Tosaut L'Ouverture" popped into my head. Unfortunately, no music popped in with it.

Still, the title wouldn't let me be. The more I thought about it the more that second syllable, "-saut," seemed intent on telling me something, something I vaguely remembered having read having to do with ring shouts. When I got home tonight I followed up on it. It took a while but I finally found what I was looking for in Lydia Parrish's book *Slave Songs of the Georgia Sea Islands*. Concerning the word "shout" (which refers not to the singing but to the circumambular movement the singing accompanies), she uses Lorenzo Turner's work on West African survivals in Gullah to suggest an Arabic provenance: "Dr. L. D. Turner has discovered that the Arabic word *Saut* (pronounced like our word 'shout'), in use among the Mohamedans of West Africa, meant to run and walk around the Kaaba." That clinched it. One black rock had led me to another. The Juaneño had led me to Mecca by way of Haiti and the Georgia coast. "Tosaut L'Ouverture," I now knew, was a piece I *had* to write. It would demand all the syncretistic salt I could muster. Exactly the sort of work I like most.

So far no good. I'm beginning to think I should change the title to "I Can't Get Started." I sat down before going to bed and tried to work something up. Nothing I came up with worked. What most readily suggested itself was a derivative tack I didn't find at all satisfactory — allusions to "Salt Peanuts," "Haitian Fight Song" and so forth. I finally gave up and went to bed but, as I've said, couldn't get to sleep. My head, it seemed, had become a black rock. I saw notes revolving around it — the notes, I took it, to the Afro-Amerindian dhikr I was after — but the hitching movement they made made it impossible to make them out.

The difficulty might be put this way: By syncretistic salt one means a mix in which adverse traditions relativize one another, relate while applying a grain of salt to one another. Though "while" need not exclude "by way of," what's hard is not to conflate the two, not to foreclose on truth however rightly one recoils from presumed absolutes. The detour thru salt, that is, isn't the same as obstruction. Nor does it argue anything goes. Relativistic salt insists upon a hitch. By way of that hitch it calls its orbit into question, laments its ability to universalize though it employs it nonetheless. Some such hitch, in some way I've yet to figure out, has to advance "Tosaut L'Ouverture."

Writing you, I thought, might help. I'm not sure it has as far as getting going on the piece is concerned, but it's done some good to put the problem in words. I'll close now and, whichever comes first, either get going or get some sleep.

Sincerely,
N.

PS: (Next day, before I mail this.) Sleep came first.

Dear Angel of Dust,

Not a whole lot of progress to report on "Tosaut
L'Ouverture," except that I've decided there'll be a synthesizer
in it. This would be a first for us, though Djamilaa's had a syn-
thesizer for a few months now and is getting to know her way
around on it pretty well. What I like is the sense of extrapola-
tive surge one can get from it, the sense of immanent atmos-
phere, spheric dilation, synaptic expanse. I'd like, running the
risk of a lapse into the programmatic, to save it for the last part
of the piece, have it come on like a sudden crystallization, a
capacious "inwardness" turned unexpectedly "overt." What I'd
like to evoke is a psychotropic surge into synthetic air, a syn-
thesized ripening of resident capacity tantamount to a "mira-
cle of the fishes" all its own — etheric, synthetic, yet (in only
the most corporeal sense) "inside," an extrapolative sense of
streaming viscera (vatic outwardness, visceral sky). This is all,
I admit, merely embryonic, a mere beginning.

Here, in any case, are some thoughts I think might move
matters further along: 1) Saltwater intransigence translates
grain of salt into grain of truth. 2) Black rock is the occult
obduracy the pursuit of granular truth revolves around. 3) By
salt one means a reminder of waters crossed. 4) Salt returns
us to ourselves, brings us back to where we were, wakes us up
to sedated senses of who we are. 5) Black salinity thrives on
the memory of cramped space, the congestion Tosaut salt
opens up.

Somewhere I want it also implied, if not stated outright,

that the swept air, the unstrapped immensity of synthesized advent, wipes away chagrin. But that's a bridge we'll cross when we get to it.

   You're well I hope.

As ever,
N.

Dear Angel of Dust,

I've been listening a lot these past few days to "Cyclic Episode," one of the cuts on *Fuchsia Swing Song*, one of Sam Rivers's early albums. Something about it seems to speak all the more pointedly to me these days, something pertinent, I can't help thinking, to "Tosaut L'Ouverture." Perhaps it's the understated way Sam has of opening it up, the way understatement works to further, of all things, the anthemlike way the piece gathers, the seemingly offhand way in which it grows. There's an air of confidentiality he lends the head's ditty-bop assurance, intimations of a ditty-bop conspiracy, some hip, whispered insurgency we sense might be afoot. It all somehow turns on that soft-spoken entrance, the way chagrin seems to've long since been dealt with, digested, qualms verged on but in the end veered away from, the head spun of an element all its own by so close an encounter. Then, too, one mustn't forget the degree to which *grow* gives way to *glide* at crucial points, only then to come back with such ferocity we see that *growl* inhered in what *grow* proposed. I'm struck, that is, by the way soft-spoken entrance opens onto its opposite, as though the likelihood of abrupt, expulsive dilation obtained at all points. I'm reminded of something of Rumi's I once read: "When you have closed your mouth on this side, open it on that, for your shout of triumph will echo in the placeless air."

What Rumi has to say bears not only on "Cyclic Episode" but also on *saut*, the unsounded shout he thus helps us to see as a two-sided shout, the circumambular play of not only voiced but unvoiced endowments. I'm wondering if this doesn't in some way have something to say about the blank I continue to draw when it comes to "Tosaut L'Ouverture." Could that blank, that is, be the unsounded side of a shout which resounds elsewhere, the unsounded side on which that elsewhere shuts me up? What I like about "Cyclic Episode" is the way Sam seems to've been able to give both sides their due. I'd avail myself of a similar ditty-bop ability to dwell in unplaced as well as placed air, unvoiced as well as voiced investiture, unbased as well as based circumlocution. This would seem to be the challenge I've not yet risen to in my attempts to tap into "Tosaut L'Ouverture," to bring it over from that other side on which I'm now even more convinced it resides. Something like Sam's unhurried assurance might be the soft-spoken key, the "open sesame," I'm after.

As I've already said, I've been listening to that one cut over and over these past few days. It got to where getting up to return the needle to where the cut begins got to be a drag, so I put it on tape in what amounts to a loop, the one cut, repeated, taking up the entire cassette. (What's more, I've got an auto reverse cassette player, so I don't even have to turn it over.) I'm listening to it now, as I write. In fact, something I heard in what went by a few moments ago I have to say something about, for it seemed if I could only reach at the appropriate angle I'd have been able to take hold of the soft-spoken entry of which the minor sevenths the piece piles up appear intent on telling, literally hold it in my hand. The hovering accretion Sam somehow manages made me think of the air of which we're thus apprised as momentarily so possible it became palpable as well, a teasing hint of tangibility I'm straining my pen to give senses of. (Words may not, as I once heard someone say, go there, but I'm convinced they do come from there.) Though Sam's ditty-bop insistences accent fugitivity, the runaway gist and the apt impropriety of any such attempt, I did in fact attempt to take hold of that air. Evidently I got the

Dear Angel of Dust,

I finally got "Tosaut L'Ouverture" written. "Cyclic Episode" turned out, as I suspected it would, to be the key, though you'd never guess the lengths I had to go to to get it to work. Have you ever heard of "Muslim soup"? Probably not. Neither had I until a few days ago when I read about a group of people known as the Nafama, a nonliterate group who live in northwestern Ghana. They've been influenced by the Mande, their Muslim neighbors, and though they've not converted to Islam they believe Arabic script has talismanic power, Koranic verses particularly so. They make a brew they call *siliama-que*, "Muslim soup." This they do by steeping roots and herbs in water used to wash Islamic chalkboards, boards on which verses from the Koran have been written being believed to make the strongest "soup." Their version of holy water, it can be sprinkled on a person to give him or her protection, but it's thought to be most effective when imbibed. They tell stories of invulnerability to bullets being thus induced.

Anyway, my frustrated attempts to get going on "Tosaut L'Ouverture" finally got to where I decided to concoct a chalkboard brew of my own, a talismanic tea or soup (*saut* soup I decided I'd call it) which would assist me toward the breakthrough I sought. What I did was write out the head to "Cyclic Episode" on a chalkboard and wash it away with water, saving the water and adding herbs and roots to make *saut* soup. I couldn't help thinking of the chalk-inscribed head as being something like a vévé in Haitian vodoun, though analogies to football or basketball (plays drawn up in chalk) seemed relevant as well. It was as I drank the chalky concoction that a further parallel suggested itself: the book John eats in *Revelation*. The stomached ordeal the bitter brew induced hit me at once. I felt I'd vomit, so queasy, so conducive to qualms had my stomach become, big with bibliophagous apprehensions it seemed, angst wound up inside it like a scroll. The watery book I'd swallowed meted out emulsified extrusions of what turned out, as in the Djeannine dream, to be emptiness, air, albeit, as in the dream, x-ray emptiness, x-ray air. I looked at my legs and saw bones, looked at my arms and saw bones, looked and saw bones and internal organs when I looked at my torso.

A ring of notes began to revolve around my head, possessed of an intimate spin as though bent (bent by the antipodal itch to hold something which had never been held before). They bobbed like horses on a carousel, made of wood but with a lifelike limberness evocative of blood warmth, heat, hot pursuit. They ran ridden by the hitch which bore them aloft, Haitian horses, winged rule and winged exception rolled into one unruly whir, intimate spur rolled in with warm, unquenchable spin. Each horse was "given its head," as though of each it could have honestly been said, "Everything I know runs within that note." Each note was a Tosaut rock, Tosaut horse, ready to break, run out from inside. Everything I knew ran around my head in a ring which grew so tight, so like a tourniquet, I was afraid my eyes would pop out. I felt as if I'd been poisoned, not unlike Ouiot, the ring of notes part would-be crown, part mark of the beast.

But such, I consoled myself, were the visionary dues one had to pay, bled by what one knew in such fashion even stanching the flow was a pain, an ordeal. The ring of notes did eventually stand still, stop turning, the only problem then being that, pressed as they were to my head, I could no longer see them, much less make them out. The ring loosened a bit, not so much a tourniquet anymore as a sweatband or a band-age, but it still didn't stand away from my head the way it had at first. To see the notes I had no recourse but to look in a mirror. I somehow made my way to the bathroom, where with the help of the mirror on the medicine cabinet I could make out the notes which girded my head, those at the back with the aid of a handheld mirror used in concert, so to speak, with the larger one.

I'm not sure I've made it clear that also girding my head was a staff and that it was on this that the notes were written. Thus it was, in any event, that I finally got going. I got out some staff paper and copied what I saw in the mirror, then got out my tenor and played what I'd written and, liking what I heard, knew "Tosaut L'Ouverture" was at last underway. It obliquely and ever so elusively recalled "Cyclic Episode," though what the resemblance consisted of one would've been extremely hardpressed to say. I've since come to see that it has somewhat the same relationship to "Cyclic Episode" that Frank Wright's "One for John" has to "Naima," except that here there's an even more teasing, immensely more lost-on-the-tip-of-the-tongue sense of (there's no other way to say it) Tosaut opening, Tosaut access.

Anyway, I got the piece written, only to run into a hitch when I took it to rehearsal. After I passed out the charts and we talked about the piece a bit, we gave it a go. Everything went okay for the first few bars but then the time began to drag, this getting worse the farther we went, my gestures to Drennette to pick up the tempo notwithstanding. Soon she quit playing altogether, saying that something about the piece deeply disabled her, that she couldn't say exactly what it was but that her legs and arms had begun to knot up, her body to ache under what felt like added weight. She immediately went on, however, to allow that this made no sense, that it must've been all in her mind, so we gave it another try but the same thing happened. Again, a few bars into the piece she stopped, complaining that her legs and arms were on the verge of cramping, that the sense of added weight had come on again. We gave it several more tries but each time the same thing happened.

We put our heads together as to what was going on. Pressed to go into it, Drennette said the piece reminded her of something she couldn't quite put her finger on, that, more specifically, it brought another piece to mind whose title escaped her. "'Cyclic Episode,'" I suggested. After a moment's reflection she said yes, that was it. This, then, cleared the whole thing up. Our best collective guess was that "Tosaut L'Ouverture's" oblique recollection of "Cyclic Episode" spoke, on some deep muscular level, to Drennette's memory of the spill she suffered on her last bike ride with Rick. Oblique namesake recall spoke not only subliminally but physically, percussive spirit bested, here at least, by traumatic spill, Tosaut opening undermined by Tosaut block. The question, then, was — and remains — what to do about it.

Let me know what you think.

Yours,

N.

most about the piece is the confluence of sympathetic and synthetic resonances Drennette and Djamilaa's interplay brings one back to again and again.

I'm enclosing a tape of the piece we made at rehearsal last night. You'll notice from the label that we've settled on a new name for the band. This came about only a few days ago, about the same time, actually, as I got your "prescription." (It seems to've been a week for solutions.) The name is a composite of two names Lambert and Aunt Nancy suggested, both of which we liked but were ultimately unable to decide between. Lambert's idea was that we call ourselves the Molimo Sound Ensemble, a name alluding to the Mbuti Pygmies of the Congo. You may have read *The Forest People*, Colin Turnbull's book about the Mbuti, and, if so, you may remember that the molimo is the name they give the ritual they perform at times of crisis, a ritual consisting mainly of songs sung nightly by the men. It's also the name given to the fire around which they gather, as well as to the musical instrument, a long trumpet, which assumes a central role in the ritual. The trumpet's voice is the voice of the forest, the voice, the men tell the women, of "the animal of the forest," a forest monster women are not allowed to see. But this assertion of male primacy and privilege gets undermined in the course of the performance Turnbull recounts. It comes to light that originally the women owned the molimo. Hence Lambert's reasoning that "Molimo Sound Ensemble" resolves Drennette and Aunt Nancy's objection to "Mystic Horn Society's" male bias. He made his reasoning clear by reading from a book by Evan Zuesse, *Ritual Cosmos*, three of whose chapters deal with the Mbuti. Zuesse refers to what he terms "the molimo spirit," a spirit of mediation or reconciliation, it turns out, characterized by a coincidence of opposites, as in the passage Lambert read to us: "The beginning of the festival seems to suggest the phallic aspect of the molimo; the end equates the molimo with the women. Actually, we may have the answer to the nature of the spirit in concluding that it is both male and female. In almost every area of symbolism the molimo is the unity of opposites."

Aunt Nancy's idea was that we call ourselves the Maatet, or, simply, Maatet, a name the Egyptians gave one of the boats in which the sun sails across the sky, the one it boards at dawn, the morning boat (the other being the one in which it completes its journey, Sektet, the evening boat). Maatet joins Atet, a more common name for the morning boat, with Maat, the name of the goddess of truth: Maat + Atet = Maatet. Aunt Nancy said she likes the suggestion of maternity, matriarchy, in the very sound of it, as well as what she calls its feminization of SunStick's claim, "I play truth." (It was at SunStick's aborted audition, remember, that we made the decision to seek a woman drummer.) She'd gotten intimations of the name, she said, a few weeks back, when we played the clamp-lilac-eelpot rendition of "Sun Ship." The glass-bottom disposition it opened up seems to've been an avatar of see-thru truth, a truth whose translucent body she rode, not yet consciously equating its light touch with Maat's ostrich feather. "Ever since then," she said, "I've had a feeling of namesake encasement, see-thru cartouche, a swift, boat-bodied lightness, light-bodied bigness we'd grow into. It's a name we'll have to fill in, occupy, but I don't have any doubts we can."

As I've said, we liked both names — though not entirely without reservations. Drennette said she thought "Molimo Sound Ensemble's" implicit critique of male bias was too implicit, too subtle, that most people would miss it. Penguin, on the other hand, said he thought "Maatet," ostrich feather notwithstanding, was a bit heavyhanded. There were some other quibbles as well, but these two were the most substantive. The former we decided to address by giving "Molimo," as though it were Spanish, an alternate, feminine ending, "-ma," adding it with the help of a slash, on the model of "his/her"— that is, Molimo/ma. This helped address Penguin's reservation as well, allowing "Maatet" to become "Atet" ("-ma Atet") in the compound/compromise "Molimo/ma Atet." We then dropped the slash, kept the space between "-mo" and "ma," closed the space between "ma" and "Atet," contracting and apostrophizing to get "m'Atet." Hence, the Molimo m'Atet.

As ever,
N.

Dear Angel of Dust,

There's a story John Gilmore tells about the first time he played in New York. It was in 1956 at Birdland, where he'd been hanging out with his horn for about a month without getting a chance to play. Pat Patrick was working there with Willie Bobo's band one night and it was thanks to him that John finally got a chance to sit in. He says he knew right away he wouldn't be able to play with them the way he was used to playing, in the loose, "lag along" Chicago style. They took a stiffer tack, so after he jumped into his solo he decided to play, as he puts it, "contra to them." He played *against* everything they played. Whatever rhythm they played he played its opposite, playing inversions instead of straight eighth or straight sixteenth notes. "Contrary motion" he calls it. He says Trane was in the audience that night and that he liked what he heard so much he came running up to him afterwards saying, "John Gilmore, John Gilmore, you've got it, you've got the concept! You've got the concept! You've got to show me how to play some of that stuff."

I bring this up in response to your kind comments on "Tosaut L'Ouverture," your request that I say a bit more regarding "cystic regard for what gets away." You're right, I think, to say that there's a poetics implied, though to call it a prosody makes the point more precisely. You're also right to relate this to the "peculiar sense of weight" you find at work in "Tosaut L'Ouverture," the galled and galling combinatory pace parsed out in rapport (parallactic rapport) with an agile array of inertial constraints. John Gilmore comes to mind because that "sense," to my ears at least, is one which flirts with unwieldiness, gives a feel for unwieldiness in ways which are indebted to my longtime fascination with his approach. I'm struck by the way the tenor, in John's hands, seems to become bulkier, bigger, more dangerous, a volatile beast requiring more effort to simply hold on to. One hears appre-hensions of imminent emergency, a strapped, struggling con-ception of things as though at all points they were on the verge of getting away, getting out of hand. He approaches the horn with a lion trainer's caution and respect, a circumspect "contrary motion" which is endlessly at pains not to be caught out. Maybe it's more an anti-prosodic than a prosodic approach, the "lag along" looseness of it insisting on a resis-tant lag, a contestatory lag, as if keeping up were a life-or-death struggle and an irrelevance both.

In any event, for "resistant lag" read "regard for what gets away," galled and galling regard. Read "stolen march," "con-testatory stagger," "lost step." I'm thinking of Alejo Carpentier's novel *The Lost Steps*, where the search for the origins of music repeatedly turns upon an insistence on fugi-tivity, a resistance to capture at even the vegetative level. ("'These are the plants which have fled from man since the beginning,' the friar told me, 'the rebel plants, those which refused to serve him as food, which crossed rivers, scaled mountains, leaped the deserts. . . .'") Thinking of the salsa group Orquesta Cimarrón, I relate this to marronage, the run-away tack resorted to by so many slaves. It's as if in our music we honor fugitive roots while paying homage to captive kin, as if, descendants of captives, we come to the beat (punctual capture, captive concurrence) with weightier qualms, weight-ier qualifications. "Lag along" equivocation speaks to this.

But I don't want to load it up entirely on rhythm. John's intonation has taught me a lot as well. You've no doubt noticed the way he endows his tone, whether in the upper or the lower register, with inklings of tenuous containment, an insinuative touch which makes us imagine a mere twitch of his lip would take the whole thing out. As with the rhythm, he appears to grapple with an extrapolative tonality, a timbral momentum which wants to work loose. Adumbrations of imminent alarm run throughout, the beginnings of a sirenlike escalation, no matter how muffled, never not implicitly there. Think of Clifton Chenier doing "I Can't Stop Loving You," how he lets the accordion begin to scream only to rein it back in, coming right out on the *Bon Ton Roulet* album and saying, "Whoa," the poignant play between "whoa" and "can't stop" addressing runaway love with resistant (would-be resistant) lag.

There's more I could go into, but this, I think, puts it in a nutshell. Thanks for your strong response to "Tosaut L'Ouverture." I hope it's true that with it, as you say, we've turned a corner.

Yours,
N.

5.VI.82

Dear Angel of Dust,

The other shoe finally dropped. We're in Seattle playing a three-night stint at a club called Soulstice. Last night, the first night of the gig, new repercussions on a number of fronts came to light. Foremost among them is that the wouldly subsidence in which Penguin and Drennette's embryonic romance had gotten hung up seems to've given way, exacting a ledge, an atomistic ledge, from the lapse it rescinded. You've no doubt noticed that since Penguin's return from Wouldly Ridge it's been as though his embryonic courtship of Drennette had never occurred. He's not only not pursued it further, he'll neither speak nor hear talk of it. Whenever I've brought it up he's acted like he had no idea what I was talking about, staring at me with a blank, uncomprehending look on his face, as though English were a foreign language, as if I spoke some unheard-of tongue. Aunt Nancy, Lambert and Djamilaa say it's been the same with them. Drennette likewise has acted like nothing ever happened. She and Penguin have been nothing but normal in their dealings with one another.

It's hard to say what it was, why it was wouldly subsidence took this occasion to exact wouldly ledge. My guess is that the air of anticlimactic futurity pervading this town had something to do with it, the datedness of what was once thought of as "things to come." I'm referring, of course, to the Space Needle. That the future has no place in which to arrive but the present, that its arrival is thus oxymoronic, is the sort of reflection one can't help entertaining in the shadow of such a monument as that — a monument, when it was built, to the future, a future it prematurely memorialized, prematurely entombed. Today it's more properly a monument to the past, a reminder of the times in which it was built, tomb to the elapsed expectancy it all turns out to've been. I remember my aunt and uncle driving up for the World's Fair twenty years ago—hopelessly long ago it seems now.

But by no means to be ignored is the reinforcement given elapsed or outmoded future by us happening to hear "Telstar," the early sixties hit by the Tornadoes, on the jukebox in a diner we had lunch in yesterday. The tinny, strained, "futuristic" sound of it said it all, spoke to a sense of lost occasion elapsed future began infusing us with the moment we laid eyes on that Needle. I thought of every wish which had seemed to miss the mark in being fulfilled, though I corrected myself at once, admitting the case to be one of an "it" which could only be projected, never arrived at. Anticlimactic "it," I reminded myself, allotted virtual space, an ironic investiture missed opportunity couldn't help but inhabit. Disappointment, the needling sense of a missed appointment, couldn't help but be there. This we knew before "Telstar" came on. We knew it all the more once it did.

The weather played a part as well. It hasn't rained outright since we've been here but it's been overcast and drizzling, a thin mist coming down pretty much all the time. That mist, it seemed, went with us into the club last night. It adopted a low profile for the occasion, close to the floor like a carpet so intimate with our feet we'd have sworn we dragged it in. What had been of the air was now oddly underfoot. In a way it was like the world had turned upside down, the way the mist, instead of falling from the sky, came up from the floor, ever so lightly addressing the soles of our feet. The difference this would make in our music was evident at once. No sooner had we taken the stage than the low-lying mist was an atomistic ledge we stood on which made our feet feel as though they'd fallen asleep—not entirely numb but (you know the feeling

I'm sure) put upon by pins, subject to a sort of pointillist embrace. Point had become a hydra, its pinpoint tactility multiply-pinned. We couldn't help knowing it was "missed" on which we stood (missed mark, missed opportunity, missed appointment), no less real, no less an actual mist even so. What it came down to was an odd, pointillist plank-walk, notwithstanding we walked in place if it can be said we walked at all. The ledge onto which we stepped calibrated a tenuous compound or compaction of low-lying spray with spreading phantasmality (phantom feet and/or the phantom ledge on which "missed" insisted we stood).

We stood on lost, oddly elevated ground, elegiac ledge. This was no mere materialization of loss even so, no glib legitimation of lack, elegy (lapsed eligibility) notwithstanding. We stood upon or perhaps had already stepped across an eccentric threshold, thrust, or so it seemed, into a post-expectant future, the anti-expectant gist of which warned us that "post-" might well turn out to've been premature. What expectant baggage did we weigh ourselves down with even now? What ingenuous out did we disingenuously harbor hopes of having secured? The needling mist which addressed our feet multiply apprised us of an inoculative boon we sought even as we disavowed all promise, all prepossessing "post-." Post-expectant futurity stood accused of harboring hope. Nonetheless we stood by it, one and all, atomistic ledge an exemplary rug allotting endless rapport, unimpeachable aplomb.

Post-expectant futurity stood its ground. It was this of which our feet grew multiply-possessed before we hit a single note. Though its multiply-pinned massage ostensibly comforted the soles of our feet, the needling mist became a goad of sorts. The quantum-qualitative lift it afforded gave an operatic lilt and leverage to the post-expectant ground on which we stood. Ground and goad rolled into one, it coaxed an abrupt, acquiescent grunt from each of our throats, an abrupt, expectorant exhalation whose fishbone urgency furthered itself once we began to play. Part seismic splint, part psychic implant exacting an auto-inscriptive lilt, it put the phrase "inasmuch as what we want is real" on the tips of our tongues, amending our attack and our intonation in ways we'd have not thought possible had it not been so palpably so. What this meant was that "want" walked arm in arm with "real" across bumptious ground. We knew it all at once, it seemed, an instantaneous jolt as though the needling mist were an electric mace.

We were several bars into our opening number before fishbone urgency let go of our throats. The ripped, expectorant permission it apprised us of abruptly left us on our own, ushered albeit we were that much farther along the pointillist plank on which we walked. Djamilaa, Penguin, Aunt Nancy, Lambert and I stood in staggered array, stumbling in place while Drennette sat as though caught in a suspended spill. She looked as if she'd fallen backwards, as if her fall had been broken by the stool on which she sat. She too, it appeared, stumbled in place.

Our collective stumble suspended us in time it seemed, notwithstanding the atomistic ledge had a decidedly glide aspect and sense of advance running thru it. This was its odd, contradictory confirmation of post-expectant premises, the odd, post-expectant way it had of rolling promise and prohibition into one. The piece we opened with was Lambert's "Prometheus." The expectorant, post-expectant permission the occasion laced it with put one in mind of Charles Davis's "Half and Half," the rash, rhythmelodic treadmill effect Elvin Jones and Jimmy Garrison's band exact on the *Illumination* album. Still, it went way beyond that in the anticlimactic refractivity, the visionary hiccup we fostered and factored in. It was this which tallied with while taking elsewhere the iterative carpet-ride on which we ran in place. Iterant weave and itinerant rug ran as one. Atomistic ledge came on as though steeped in deep-seated conveyance, *run* so deeply woven into wouldly arrest it was all we could do to keep our feet on the floor. The conveyor-belt bridge and the bedouin breach it addressed introduced a deep, irredentist quiver to the needling mist, an ever so agitant feather's touch tickling our feet.

What struck us most was how quickly we'd moved onto mixed-metaphorical ground. Where was it we stood if stand could be said to be what we did? Where was it we stumbled if stumble said it better? So many different sensations complicated one another: mixed-metaphorical conveyor-belt/carpet-ride, mixed-metaphorical mist/pointillist plank, mixed-metaphorical feather/pinpoint massage, mixed-metaphorical splint/low-lying spray. . .

The other shoe I spoke of to begin with fully partook of this dispensation, a mixed-metaphoricality which brought off being a hammer, a broken pedal and a shoe at the same time. It seemed a Cinderella fit or effect wherein hammer, broken pedal and shoe were now showcase items, encased in or even constituted of glass. Hammer had been placed under glass by the Penny dream. Broken pedal had been placed under glass by Drennette's concussive spill, shoe (slipper, to be more exact) by the presumption of fairy-tale artifice, fairy-tale fit. These three were one, a see-thru insistence upon breakage, atomization, the meaning, however chimeric, of atomistic ledge. The other shoe, the newly shod alterity onto which or into which or invested with which we now stepped, came down with a resounding report it took us a while to realize was us — a new sound which, unbeknown to ourselves, we'd come up with (or which, "unbeknown" being the case, had come up with us).

Other shoe mixed-metaphorically segued into other shore, the floor sliding away like sand when a wave retreats. Suppositious wave, I turned around and saw, was intimated, ever so exactly meted out, by the drumroll Drennette now sustained, a roll which required all but acrobatic skill, so at odds with the suspended spill it appeared she was in. Suppositious retreat, the spasmic thumps thrown in on bass drum, tended to be consistent with suspended spill, suppositious wave rolling back upon itself so as to pull what ground one thought there was back with it. Thus it was that Drennette played out the mixed-emotional endowment her final bicycle ride with Rick had left her with, the promise and the putting aside of promise her critique of "antique emotion" so insisted on. Promise and resistance to promise rolled pregnancy and post-expectancy into one, the bass drum pedal sounding the post-expectant "floor" the broken pedal had introduced her to.

Drennette's anti-foundational patter recalled the fact (recalled while commenting on the fact) that it was Lambert's debut of "Prometheus" which had launched us on our quest for a drummer. Whatever hope he might have had of bedrock solidity had long since been given an antithetic spin, made to comply with and to confirm or anticipate (or so it seemed in retrospect) the sense of anticlimactic futurity we've been under since getting here. The rhythmic anchor Lambert announced he wanted had turned out to be exactly that, turned out to be a *rhythmic* anchor. Rhythmicity, Drennette insisted, contends with bedrock foundation, the sense of an unequivocal floor anchorage implies.

That the atomistic ledge on which we stood entailed wouldly subsidence having been rescinded became clear the more one listened to Penguin. The piece's "love slave" thematics, the subtextual strain having to do with Epimetheus's "hots" (as Penguin put it) for Pandora, was the thread he pulled out and pursued. It took us a while to realize it, but this was largely what was new about the way we sounded. Never before had we so equated Promethean fire with Epimethean "hots." While at first it was difficult to pick out Penguin's advancement of that equation from the avalanche of sound we put forth, his needling insinuation that "Pandora" was an apter title than "Prometheus" gradually came to the fore. Gradually he blew louder, needling insinuation becoming more blunt, less innuendo than hammerlike assertion. The more assertive he became the more Drennette encouraged the equation he advanced, quickening the pace with rabbit-like rolls as though they were wheels for him to ride. Penguin, in turn, grew bolder, swifter, quickening the pace to play Epimetheus to what he took to be Drennette's Pandora (or took, it turned out, to be Djeannine's Pandora, took to be Drennette's Djeannine).

It was a blistering pace which Penguin handled without the slightest loss of articulacy. With each note he did as he wished. He clearly had something to say, something which all but leapt out of him, so Lambert and I backed away from our mikes, letting him solo first. Drennette's rabbitlike rolls continued to feed the Epimethean heat with which he blew, heat which was all the more astonishing considering the finesse with which he played, the nuanced ability to speak which, notwithstanding the frenzy it appeared he was in, he maintained. His oboe spoke. It not only spoke but did so with outrageous articulacy, so exquisitely so a balloon emerged from its bell. Lambert and I looked at one another. We traded looks with Aunt Nancy, Djamilaa and Drennette as well. It was hard to believe one's eyes but there it was, a comic-strip balloon enclosed in which one read the words Penguin's oboe spoke: *Drennette dreamt I lived on Djeannine Street. I walked from one end to the other everyday, back and forth all day. Having heard flamenco singers early on, I wanted in on duende.* Penguin took a breath and with that the balloon disappeared.

Another balloon took the first balloon's place when Penguin blew again, a balloon in which one read: *A long-toed woman, no respecter of lines, Drennette obliged me by dreaming I walked up and down Djeannine Street, stepping, just as she or Djeannine would, into literality, notwithstanding the littered sidewalk and the unkempt yards.* He took another breath and when he blew again the third balloon read: *Sprung by her long toe, Drennette (part gazelle, part tumbleweed) leapt away as I reached out to embrace Djeannine. Among the weeds in a vacant lot a half-block away, she ran a few steps and turned a cartwheel. All I wanted was to bury my head between her legs, press my nose to the reinforced crotch of her white cotton panties.* He took another breath and when he blew again the fourth balloon read: *Something I saw, thought I saw, some intangible something led me on. Something I saw not so much as in some other way sensed, an audiotactile aroma, the synaesthetic perfume Djeannine wore which was known as Whiff of What Was, a scent like none I'd otherwise have known.*

While this fourth balloon hung in the air several people in the audience stood up and came forward to get a better look, not stopping until they stood in front of Penguin, squinting to make out the last few words. I had already noticed that *a* and *scent* were written somewhat close together, so I took it they were trying to determine whether what was written was *a scent* or *ascent.* They returned to their seats when Penguin took another breath and the fourth balloon disappeared. In its place, when he blew again, was a fifth which read: *The salty-sweet, sweating remembrance of Drennette's long-toed*

advance animated the street with an astringent allure, a rut-
tish funk I fell into which was more than mere mood.
Drennette's advance made the ground below the sidewalk
swell, cracking the concrete to release an atomistic attar, dilat-
ing my nostrils that much more.

This went on for some time, a new balloon appearing each
time Penguin blew after taking a breath. There was a sixth, a
seventh, an eighth balloon and more. How many there were
in all I can't say. I lost count. In any case, I understood them
as a ploy by way of which Penguin sought to gain relief, comic
relief, from the erotic-elegiac affliction of which the oboe so
articulately spoke. By way of the balloons he made light of
and sought to get leverage on the pregnant, post-expectant
ground Drennette so adamantly espoused or appeared to
espouse. The leverage he sought gave all the more torque to
the dream-projection he projected onto her, the "street" he
later admitted to be based on the projects he lived in as a
child. There was a regal touch to it as well, each balloon both
cartoon and cartouche, this latter aspect very much in keep-
ing with the stately tone the oboe wove into its erotic-elegiac
address. Wounded kingship came thru loud and clear, an
amalgam of majesty and misery, salty-sweet. Love lost was as
easily loss loved it intimated, a blasé spin the blue funk it
announced increasingly came to be amended by. Such grim
jest or indifferent gesture increasingly infiltrated courtly
ordeal, cap and bells inaugurating an alternate crown, King
Pen's cartoon/cartouche. Laughing to keep from crying some
would call it, but in fact it went much deeper than that.

Penguin wrapped up his solo with a round of circular
breathing which introduced an unexpected wrinkle to what
had by then become a pattern: blow/balloon emerge, take
a breath/balloon disappear, blow/balloon emerge, take a
breath/balloon disappear, blow/balloon emerge, take a

breath/balloon disappear. . . The breath he now took was continuous with the one he expelled and the balloon, instead of disappearing, hung in the air above the bell of his horn growing larger the longer he blew. The steady enlargement, however, was only partly what was new about the new wrinkle he introduced. Two-dimensional up to this point, the balloon acquired a third dimension as it grew, becoming a much more literal balloon. What was also new was that there were now no words written inside it. By making it more a literal than a comic-strip balloon Penguin put aside the comic lever he'd made use of up to this point. He was now nothing if not emotionally forthright, the empty balloon all but outright insisting, the way music so often does, that when it came to the crux of the matter, the erotic-elegiac fix one was in, words were beside the point.

The admission that words fail us would normally not have been so unexpected, normally come as no surprise. Music, as I've said, does it all the time. But in this case it seemed a new and unusual twist, so persuasively had the comic-strip balloons insisted it could all be put into words. It's a measure of Penguin's genius that he could endow something so close to cliché with new life. The balloon not only swelled like a pregnant belly but, thanks to the mixed-metaphorical ground onto which we'd moved, it appeared to be a sobriety-test balloon as well. Penguin blew into it intent on proving himself sober even as he extolled the intoxicant virtues of Djeannine's audiotactile perfume. Whiff of What Was notwithstanding, the vacant balloon seemed intended to acquit him of drunken charges, the admission of words' inadequacy a sobering descent from the auto-inscriptive high to which the earlier balloons had lent themselves. Even so, this descent could easily be said to have been further flight, so deciduously winged was the winded ferocity with which Penguin blew, what falling off there was reaching beyond itself with a whistling falsetto—stratospheric screech and a crow's caw rolled into one.

So it was that sobering descent mounted higher and higher. The balloon grew bigger and bigger, a weather balloon pitting post-expectant wind against pregnant air. Penguin put a punning spin on it, wondering out loud whether it might also be the other way around, pregnant wind encountering post-expectant air. With us crescendoing behind him all the while (Lambert and I had now joined back in), he eventually answered his own question when the balloon swelled and swelled and finally burst with a loud bang, pricked by a post-expectant needle, the needling mist which was now not only on the floor. It was with this that he brought his solo to an end, whereupon the audience went crazy, loudly applauding the release he'd had them hungering for, the release he now at last let them have.

Penguin timed it exactly right. The audience couldn't have stood another beat, much less another bar, couldn't have held its collective breath a moment longer. We too, the rest of us in the band, breathed easier now, inwardly applauded the release we too had begun to be impatient for. All of us, that is, except Drennette, who quickly apprised us, with the solo she now insisted upon taking, of the fact that the ground on which we stood was, if anyone's, hers, that impatience had no place where post-expectancy ruled.

Post-expectant futurity brought one abreast of the ground, Drennette announced, annulled, in doing so, any notion of ground as not annexed by an alternate ground. This was the pregnancy, the unimpatient expectancy, she explained, Penguin, albeit put upon and perplexed, had been granted rare speech, rare fluency by. Djeannine Street, alternate ground par excellence, inflected each run of heavy bass drum thumps with ventriloquial spectres, Drennette's recourse to

the sock cymbal insistent that she and Djeannine, long spo-
ken for, had spooked (her word was "inspirited") wouldly
ledge, atomistic ledge.

It was a wild, outrageous boast, but she had the chops, it
turned out, to back it up. The drumset had become a wind
instrument by the time she finished her solo. A gust of wind
arose from each roll and with each roll the storm she brewed
grew more ferocious. We felt it at our backs when we joined
in again, pressing as it pestered us toward some occult articu-
lation only Drennette, not looking ahead, saw deep enough to
have inklings of. Not so much needling as pounding us now,
the needling mist partook of that wind — mystical hammer
rolled into one with atomistic pulse. Wouldly ledge, needling
mist and Penguin's auto-inscriptive high would all, post-
expectancy notwithstanding, turn out to have only been a
beginning.

Suffice it to say we made some of the most ontic, unheard-
of music we've ever made. Say what one will about unimpa-
tient expectancy, I can't wait to play again tonight.

As ever,
N.

Dear Angel of Dust,

We're back in L.A. Got back from Seattle a few days ago. The Soulstice gig, all in all, went well, though the last two nights were a little bit disappointing. It's not that we didn't play well or that the music wasn't well received. We played with fluency and fire both nights and both nights the crowd, noticeably larger than the first night, got into it, urged us on. Even so, the post-expectant ground we stepped onto the first night was nowhere to be found on nights two and three. The pointillist tread, the wouldly "one step beyond" with which we'd been blessed, pointedly avoided us the next two nights. No atomistic plank-walk lay before us, no needling mist massaged our feet. It was ground we couldn't get back to no matter how hard we tried, ground we couldn't get back to perhaps because of how hard we tried.

The most conspicuous difference was that no balloons emerged from Penguin's horn. It was this which left the audience a bit disappointed, notwithstanding the applause and the hip exhortations they repeatedly gave the music. Word of the balloons had quickly gotten around town after night number one and it was this which in large part accounted for the larger turnout the next two nights. Clearly, people came hoping to see the balloons emerge again. Though we've never thought of ourselves as crowd-pleasers, never been overly concerned with approbation, we'd have been happy to oblige them had it been up to us. But that the balloons didn't emerge amounted to an anti-expectant lesson which, while not exactly the same, was consistent with the post-expectant premises onto which we had stepped and again hoped to step. The air of anticipation the audience brought with them was so

thick that before our final number the second night, the bal-
loons not having reappeared and, clearly, to us in the band,
not likely to, Aunt Nancy stepped forward and spoke into the
mike. "Remember what Eric said," she admonished them.
"'When you hear music, after it's over, it's gone in the air. You
can never capture it again.'"

It was a lesson we ourselves have had to ponder. Post-
expectant ground was clearly evaporative ground, but it was
hard not to be disappointed we couldn't find it again. It had
been a lapse to expect otherwise we admitted, but that's been
easier to say than to accept. Lambert, in any event, said it best
as we were discussing this at rehearsal the other night. "It's
about digesting what you can't swallow," he said at one point.

As ever,

N.

Dear Angel of Dust,

Penguin phoned Lambert and me early this morning, insisting we three get together, saying there was something he needed to discuss. He asked if Lambert and I could come to his place, explaining that he was a bit shaky after what had happened. What had happened, he promised, he would go into when we got there, but he preferred not to talk about it over the phone. Lambert and I each said okay, despite the early hour, hearing something awry, the note of urgency in Penguin's voice. We got there at more or less the same time, Lambert arriving a minute or two before I did. His car was already there as I drove up. He had already gone inside.

The air of disarray hit me as soon as I walked thru the door. The house was filled with cigarette smoke. Penguin, who doesn't smoke, sat at the kitchen table smoking a cigarette, a saucer full of butts in front of him, Lambert seated at the table as well. I joined them at the table after minimal greetings and Penguin got right to the point. He had dreamt the Penny dream after falling asleep on Drennette's couch last night he said. He asked if Lambert and I had dreamt it as well. When we answered no he sighed and said, "I didn't think so." He said he felt more strongly than ever that there's more to Drennette than meets the eye, snuffing out the cigarette in the saucer of butts and immediately lighting another. "Let me begin at the beginning," he said, going on to relate why he had gone over to Drennette's. After everyone had packed up and left rehearsal, he explained, he saw the leather bag she keeps her drumsticks in lying on the floor underneath a chair. "I gave her a call to tell her she'd forgotten it," he said, pausing to take a drag on the cigarette. A wrought, whimsical look came over his face. "Maybe I had it coming, maybe I was asking for it," he allowed when he resumed talking, going on to relate how he had insisted on taking the bag to her, insisted it would be no trouble when she protested he needn't go to the trouble of driving across town. The phrase "go to the trouble" had come back to haunt him, he confessed, blowing smoke out of his nose and mouth.

Lambert and I listened in silence, despite the pauses Penguin took, no matter how lengthy. We gave him the room he so obviously needed, room enough to say what he had to say at his own pace, tell what he had to tell as best he could. He spoke with increasing deliberateness, as though the effort exacted a growing toll. It seems, in any case, he made the drive across town in record time, getting to Drennette's evidently sooner than she expected. She came to the door dressed in sweats and immediately asked him to excuse her appearance, explaining that at home she dresses for comfort rather than looks and that she had intended to put on something more presentable before he arrived. She invited him in and he handed her the drumstick bag and she asked him to have a seat. He sat on the couch and she followed suit, he at one end, she at the other. They made small talk — nervous talk, he admitted. He recalls the light being on the dim side, turned low, though he allowed that this might merely have been the fuzziness of recollection. He also recalls, more definitively, that the radio was on. "To make a long story short," he said, snuffing out the cigarette and lighting up another, "we gradually felt a bit more relaxed and she asked if I'd like a glass of wine. I said yes and she got up and when she came back she carried a bottle and two glasses. Things got more relaxed after that—eventually, it turned out, *too* relaxed."

Penguin took lengthy, forceful drags on the cigarette, sucking on it like a suffocating man trying to get air. Lambert and

I, every now and then, looked at one another out of the corners of our eyes, noting the inordinate strain he increasingly invested in each drag. He went on, between strenuous puffs, to explain that he and Drennette ended up drinking more and more wine, that they slowly and ever more relaxedly sipped several glasses, that in fact she had to open a second bottle. Their conversation, he said, flowed more and more smoothly, the nervousness and awkward talk giving way to "the most incredible, entrancing meeting of minds I've ever known." He described the conversation as "bordering on telepathic," though he admitted he couldn't recall what it was they talked about, let alone anything he or she specifically said. "In a sense," he explained, "it wasn't about words at all. It's as if we spoke in spite of the words. The words were no more than an accoutrement under which the real communication — nuance, insinuation, body language, nonverbal rapport — went its way, more or less autonomous." What he most remembers, he went on, is the extraordinary closeness, the "almost caressive receptivity" he and Drennette addressed one another with. "Indeed," he added, letting the smoke lazily cascade from his mouth, "we sat closer and closer to one another."

The going now seemed to get more difficult, the telling more a test of Penguin's ability not to break down. He spoke in a now laconic, now headlong, now herky-jerk fashion, put upon by an accumulative chagrin. He said the closeness, the caressive receptivity, was infinitely comforting, soothing, ultimately soporific. "I don't know," he said, invisibly throwing his hands up in the air. "Maybe it was the wine, perhaps the low lights (if they were in fact low), perhaps the low, confidential tone our voices assumed, the music on the radio even. Maybe it was all these things together or none of them at all. Maybe it was something I haven't thought of yet, something I may

never think of." He paused long enough to snuff out the cig-
arette and light up another. He resumed speaking by saying
that the closeness, the intimacy, the caressive receptivity, was
of such palpable presence as to project the imminence of
something more physical, that he had the feeling Drennette
wanted him to kiss her, that, whatever the case, he couldn't
help wanting to kiss her. "Our faces couldn't have been more
than two inches apart when it happened," he sighed. "I also
remember very distinctly what was on the radio. They were
playing 'Funk Underneath,' one of the things Rahsaan did
with Jack McDuff. The exhortative insistence of Rahsaan's
throaty flute is the last thing I recall being aware of."

Penguin fell silent. He seemed to assume Lambert and I
knew what "it" was, the "it" of "when it happened." It was the
lengthiest pause to that point, so lengthy we wondered was
that the end, would he go on. Finally, Lambert, impatient,
said, "Well? What happened?" Penguin started, as if awak-
ened from a trance. He took a drag on the cigarette, blew out
the smoke and related with an exasperated sigh what "it" was.
On the very verge of initiating a kiss, it turns out, he fell
asleep. He not only fell asleep; he slept for a long time, in the
course of which he dreamt the Penny dream. "It was exactly
the way Aunt Nancy and Djamilaa described it," he elabo-
rated, "except at the end." He went on to explain that rather
than concluding with the bit about a twitch in the eye and a
hole in time, as in Djamilaa's version, or with the business of
an eye made of opera glass, as in Aunt Nancy's, he found him-
self holding a spyglass up to his eye as the quarters cascaded
from the ain'thropologist's empty sockets and Penny contin-
ued pounding the floor. He couldn't, he said, believe what he
saw. Pulling away from the spyglass, he shook his head as if
to clear it, but to no avail. He saw the same scene again upon
looking thru the glass, whereupon he pulled away again, shak-

ing the spyglass rather than his head this time. At that point
the ain'thropologist, quarters cascading from his empty sock-
ets notwithstanding, spoke. "Shake it, but don't break it," he
said. "Without giving it so much as a moment's thought,"
Penguin went on, "I shot back immediately, ridiculously, 'It's
ass, not glass.' Then I woke up."

He woke up to find himself alone on Drennette's couch.
He had been asleep for several hours. Dawn was breaking.
Draped over him was a blanket Drennette had evidently cov-
ered him with. He'd apparently remained sitting the whole
time he slept. The two wine bottles, one of them empty, the
other near empty, were still on the coffee table in front of
him, as were the two glasses from which he and Drennette
had drank. "I don't know why, maybe I've seen too many
movies," he allowed, pausing to take a drag on the cigarette,
"but I picked up each glass and sniffed it. I didn't have any
trouble remembering where I was or what had brought me
there. My head was as clear as a bell, albeit the fact of having
fallen asleep the way I did made me shiver with embarrass-
ment." So much so, he went on to say, that he couldn't bear to
face Drennette, who evidently had gotten up and gone to bed
rather than wake him. All he wanted was to get out of there
as fast as he could, which is what he did, driving home in a
state of increasing dismay, a state of mind which grew increas-
ingly distraught.

"It would have been bad enough," Penguin lamented, "had
I simply fallen asleep. The fact that I dreamt the Penny dream
was even worse. But what bothers me most is the new wrinkle,
the alternate ending I introduced, the 'Shake it, but don't
break it' / 'It's ass, not glass' exchange. I know exactly where
that came from." He now got up to put water on for coffee,
asking Lambert and me would we like some, to which we both
said yes. He continued talking as he went about getting the

coffee made. He went on to tell us something we already knew, that "Shake it, but don't break it" was something which, when younger, one would say to a passing girl, referring to the way she swung her hips. She would answer, "It's ass, not glass." "It always got to me," Penguin explained, "that they would put it that way. As though ass wasn't an entity, a thing, wasn't, to put it bluntly, the butt. 'It's ass, not glass.' As though ass was a substance, even a condition, a state, atmospheric even — pervious, pervasive, diffuse — even though the tight, compact containment of it stood right there before one's eyes." He paused, as if to get a grip on himself, as if merely thinking about it, talking about it, was enough to get to him, take him out. "It made it more abstract, but all the more erotic, intensified its allure, the play between ass, put so, and blunt butt — the inordinacy, the incommensurateness of it."

Penguin now proceeded to delve deeper into the dream, especially the alternate ending he'd introduced. No hermeneutic stone was left unturned as he teased out the implications and insinuations to be found in it. Worked up, he went on and on, pursuing one interpretive tack after another. He worked it, worried it, wrung every drop of meaning he could from it. He made one think of Lee Morgan and Freddie Hubbard's version of "Pensativa" on *The Night of the Cookers*, the way they light into it and stay on it, picking at it from all angles, refusing to let it rest, pulling out strand after strand of ramification. Still, that looking is made of what one sees was the tautologic truth he couldn't get beyond. What bothered him, got to him, egged him on, was the dream's insistence that he looked at the world with a carnal eye — "not," as he put it, "a glass eye but an ass eye." The dream had him confessing that, for all his talk of there being more to Drennette than meets the eye, the delicate instrument he took himself to be saw no more than blunt butt. Shaken glass, breakable glass, the extended eye thru which he looked and the delicate projection of himself he proposed, turned out to be tantamount to swung rump.

Lambert and I, as I've already said, deferred to Penguin's need to talk, the therapeutic pursuit his going on as he did so unmistakably was. His talk was more agitated now, less prone to pauses, but whereas earlier he had made nothing in the way of overtures for us to join in, he now peppered and punctuated what he had to say by asking, "What do you think? Does that make any sense to you?" and the like. Still, we could only, whether we agreed or disagreed with him, do so in the fewest possible words (a nod of the head or a shaking of the head most often), so quickly was he off and going again. We found ourselves cut off more than a few times — whenever, that is, we tried to get more than our small allotment in. Lambert, I could see, was getting more and more annoyed at this, though Penguin didn't seem to notice. Finally, he refused to be cut off any longer and took an aggressive tack, intruding, with butt-bluntness, on Penguin's increasingly abstruse ruminations. "Why don't you and Drennette just hop in the sack and get it over with?" he snapped.

Penguin, visibly thrown off-balance, missed a beat or two but shot back, "It's not about that," immediately correcting himself by adding, "Not only about that." He would not be backed into a corner by butt-bluntness. He now spoke with less agitation in fact, as if Lambert's intervention freed him of the need to go on so, as if going on so had been a flight from butt-bluntness, a flight Lambert's intervention made it pointless to pursue, no longer possible to pursue. It was almost as if Lambert had *relieved* him of the need to go on so, so relaxedly did he take to a new pace — a slower, more open pace which made room for conversation. Penguin, though he didn't say so outright, had gotten Lambert's point.

Lambert lightened up as well. No, Penguin wasn't making a mountain out of a molehill, he allowed. Yes, these were odd goings-on. There was indeed, he admitted, more to Drennette than meets the eye, but wasn't that, he went on, the case with everyone? Any such "more," he maintained, wasn't something delving deeper into the dream would do much to get to. I also had a few things to say. We kicked it around for a while. Lambert and I both tried to convince Penguin that he should be talking to Drennette rather than talking to us, but I'm not sure we had any real success. He agreed with us readily enough—maybe too readily—but not with much resolve to actually speak with her. It was clear he's afraid to face her again. That'll change, given time, no doubt, but for now she's got him spooked. It was all we could do to talk him out of going off on another retreat.

                              Yours,
                              N.

_____18.VI.82

Dear Angel of Dust,

Drennette says that what went on the other night is that Penguin drank too much. She says he drank much, much more than she did, that he poured himself glass after glass of wine and that she wasn't surprised when he nodded off. She says it seemed he might have already had a drink or two before he got there, that he seemed nervous and worked up and must have taken a drink before coming over, trying to calm himself down. Coming over seems to have been a momentous event for him, she says, something he felt he needed fortification for, a drink or two to steady his nerves. She told this to Aunt Nancy and Djamilaa and Djamilaa told me. Djamilaa says Drennette spoke with a practiced numbness, nonchalant, saying that Penguin seemed to be in a world of his own and that she had no idea why he'd made her out to be some sort of mystery, some sort of muse. His going on about there being more to her than meets the eye she dismissed as "wine talk." "The bottle," she says, "blurs his vision."

Odd, isn't it? It's as if the post-expectant ground we happened onto in Seattle was premonitory ground. Penguin's sobriety-test balloon seems to have anticipated Drennette's flat, no-nonsense dismissal, her deflation of his enchantment with her, the charge of drunkenness her version of what went on the other night amounts to. Was Whiff of What Was a whiff of what would be? Is that even the question so much as was it a perfume or a vintage bouquet? It's an old story—he said, she said—but I tend to believe them both. It was wine Penguin got a whiff of, wine as well as perfume. But the bouquet in question, the bouquet which took Penguin out, wasn't that of the wine he and Drennette drank. The bouquet which mingled with Drennette's perfume, sweats notwithstanding, ushered in by Rahsaan's "Funk Underneath," was of a wine bottled so far back as to be ageless, wine served in the Shard Café.

It's a case of More-Than-Meets-The-Eye meets What-You-See-Is-What-You-Get. Penguin and Drennette comprise a match made in heaven: flat, post-expectant sobriety wooed by wind-afflicted high, epiphanic flight. What the outcome will be is anyone's guess.

As ever,
N.

Dear Angel of Dust,

We've had to cancel a couple of rehearsals the past few days. Penguin wasn't up to facing Drennette for a while. He's gotten over it now and things are more or less back to normal, though it's not that that I'm writing you about. I don't think I've mentioned, what with everything else that's been going on, that we've begun to move on the idea of cutting a record. We've checked out some studios around town and the money it'll take to get it done looks to be within reach. It'll be our own production, on our own label called Disques m'Atet (a foreign-sounding name should help sales), and we'll get it distributed thru New Music Distribution Service, along with mail-order ads in *Coda*, *Cadence* and the like. It'll be a while still, but we've taken the first few steps at least.

I'm enclosing a new after-the-fact lecture/libretto, "So Dja Seh," a new movement (or at least a new moment) in the antithetic opera I've been working toward. The prospect of cutting a record has made me think of "more than meets the eye" in another light, a "mediumistic" light having to do with audiotactile propensities which de-prioritize the eye, synaesthetic ascendancies of sound and scent of the sort suggested by "funk." It's been something of an elegiac reflection, recognizing that sound more and more doesn't matter, that to more and more people "more than meets the eye" makes no sense. Archie Shepp's been going around calling Michael Jackson "the Coltrane of our time," saying that nowadays it's the image, not the sound, that counts. The recent advent of "music television," visual support to an auditivity understood as insufficient, makes that abundantly clear. Djamilaa calls it "videocy."

An anthropologist once told me that Victor Turner's notion of ritual as a mechanism whereby the obligatory is made to look desirable says more about the society Turner lives in than about the Ndembu, his ostensible subject. MTV bears this out. What are music videos but consumption rituals, soft-porn commercials promoting the purchase of the very thing they help diminish, non-visual capacity, "blind" capacity (funk underneath)? Purchase of in lieu of purchase upon. Loss of non-visual capacity, audiotactility understood as lack (less than meets the eye), is the axiomatic obligation lubricating the exchange. Video insists upon a deficit in order to fill it, gives and takes at the same time: obligatory lack, illusory restitution.

Think of "So Dja Seh" as antithetic video, synaesthetic video, one in which "an eye made of opera glass" turns out to be a post-expectant picture tube. Obligatory respect for what gets away — what gets away from visualization itself — promotes a regard for what can only be off-screen, something like the quantum charade or shape-shift which defies illustration (particle/wave). Soft-porn premises, along with soft etymologic focus, blur the line between *off-screen* and *obscene*.

Yours,

N.

SO DJA SEH

*or, The Creaking of the Word: After-the-Fact
Lecture/Libretto (Drennette Virgin)*

ACT ONE

Penny wondered was it a dream the way the mist came
down like a diffuse hammer, a dream how the hammer's head,
blunt but exploded, unlike a hammer came down so gently
she moaned. She lay in bed in her room at Hotel Didjeridoo.
She knew it never snowed down under, but no sooner had she
dismissed the thought of the mist coming down like a diffuse
hammer than she thought of it as coming down like snow. No
sooner did she dismiss this thought than she thought of it as
coming down like ash.

This had to be someone's doing Penny thought. In tele-
pathic touch only the day before with her sister Djeannine liv-
ing in Djibouti, she decided that someone had to be her. Why
would Djeannine do such a thing, she wondered, just as what
sounded like a bass trombone hit a note so low it made the
windows rattle.

There was always music at Hotel Didjeridoo — mostly no
more than an all but inaudible background growl or hum, but
on occasion it rose, as it did now, in volume as well as intensity,
an insistent, insinuative thread or threnodic complaint which
told of loss, laceration, collapse. The low note, however, was
hit not by a bass trombone but by the hotel's namesake axe. It
initiated a riff one could only call doo-wop didjeridoo, a funky-
sweet rhythmic foray into ditty-bop dreamtime.

Penny wondered again was it a dream the way the mist
came down — hammer, snow, ash, the way it was all three of
them alternating one by one. Let it be said I saw it all wear

skirt. The skirt was a short one, hem at about mid-thigh, and she sat relaxed, her legs nonchalantly parted—not flagrantly so, albeit open enough to reveal a bit of her panties. This one saw, however, only after lifting a parakeet feather which had been taped to the photograph—taped at an angle between her legs, covering what little could be seen of her crotch. It was the recollection of this feather which now brought out the bird in Penguin, brought out the beak with which he bit Penny's inner thigh. He thought of his pursuit of marsupial warmth as a return to basics: feather and fur. Florid perfume, pubic funk and recollected feather worked him into a frenzy.

Penguin and Penny were conceptually complicit, giving birth to a feathered-furred amalgam which olfactorily included fish attributes as well. Furred-fish-alighted-on-by-feather spoke to their need for an annunciative mix, a new day which would contend with realist constriction, realist constraint. "The wing praises the root by taking to the limbs" was the motto inscribed above the entrance to the hotel. Both Penny and Penguin thought of it as endorsing the way he now addressed her leg, taking to it by applying namesake beak to soft inner thigh. The motto lent itself to the need for flight in which they were caught up, the need which had brought them to the hotel. It was a need to plumb depths even as one flew, to probe roots as though *plume* and *plumb* shared a common origin. "Plumbage" named a neologistic mix of which furred-fish-alighted-on-by-feather was the announcement. Hence the low note announcing ditty-bop dreamtime.

Penny's moans blended in with the music — so much so that, in a flash, before she could stop herself, she imagined Penguin had lifted his head from between her legs to ask what tune was it she was humming. Quick enough to keep from answering, however, she saw that this was only her mind playing games with her. "I'm not humming, I'm moaning" was on the tip of her tongue, but she opened her eyes and saw Penguin's head still between her thighs just in time to hold it back. Again she thought of Djeannine, that it had to be her behind this, that even Djibouti wasn't far enough away to keep Djeannine from trying to spoil her fun. The flash which had just come over her, she was convinced, was only so much telepathic noise, telepathic static, Djeannine up to no good again.

Having herself had an aborted fling with Penguin, a fledgeling affair which had never quite gotten off the ground, Djeannine, Penny suspected, resented her and Penguin having hit it off. She was now doing whatever she could to interfere, abusing the telepathic sisterly rapport which kept them in touch to make Penny's mind play games with her. Even as Penny thought this, the incongruous, disconcerting image of a penguin perched on the branch of a tree popped into her head, an outrageous reading of "wing . . . taking to the limbs" which played mercilessly upon Penguin's namesake winglessness. Such thoughts and such images were clearly meant to distract her, to destroy the mood, to make Penguin's address of her inner thigh more problematic than pleasurable. It took an effort to shoo them away but she did, moaning all the more loudly to sustain the mood.

Penny's thoughts and momentary discomposure unbeknown to him, Penguin let go of the flesh between his teeth and went back to licking, leaving her left inner thigh to attend to the right after a moment or two. Eventually, having licked and nuzzled the right for some time, he went back and forth between right and left, increasingly possessed by the pungent musk which, "part flower / part rutting beast" (as he had once read in a poem), pervaded the bed, the room, the entire world it increasingly seemed. The increased warmth of Penny's loins and crotch bore the odor aloft. Marsupial warmth, for all its

fur evocation, might as well have evoked feather instead.
What it did was endow the odor with wings, broadcasting it
about, bruiting it about, to where it did indeed fill, if not the
world, the entire room.

Broadcasting-bruiting was the way Penguin thought of it,
confounding the smell with the music which also filled the
room. Broadcasting-bruiting's endowment of wings was
indebted to, if not descended from, the parakeet feather
which had been taped to the photograph of Penny, the pubic
feather which, more than any other single item, had gotten
his and Penny's romance off the ground. It was also indebted
to doo-wop didjeridoo's winged invitation to arrive at plume
thru "plumbage," the rummaging way in which austral bird,
one way or another, would find its way to marsupial warmth.
The low note's annunciative mix of olfactory fish and marsu-
pial fur with southern flight fueled as it frustrated Penguin's
wish to translate scent into synaesthetic sound.

Penguin's tongue stroked the beginnings of pubic hair
along Penny's loins, gesturing towards without venturing into
the mound of hair and the glistening lips underneath. The
evanescent whiff of which the low note had spoken grew
endowed with everlasting allure, an amalgam of tease and
tentativeness Penguin attempted to emulate in so restrainedly
tending toward Penny's cunt. This, though, he persisted in
thinking of as her cleft. Lingering allure bred by evanescent
access instilled a wary, almost worshipful regard for what
Penguin feared would be taken away if too hurriedly pursued.
Circumlocutory "cleft" bespoke this fear no less than did the
tentative approach to it he took.

It also veiled a musical conceit. Penguin's wish to fuse
music and vaginal musk equated cleft with clef, bass clef, cleft
and key rolled into one, anagrammatic odor bound up with
anagrammatic door. Synaesthetic odor, the low note's allure,

spoke of liminal entry, limbed in-betweenness, anagrammatic fissures, cracks, namesake word-creak.°

· It befit love in a language-conscious age that he increasingly felt his arms to be fins, namesake fins, anagrammatically related to synaesthetic sniff. He part swam, part flew in the heady space between Penny's legs.

ACT TWO

Djeannine only had eyes for Djibouti. All her life she had wanted to go there. Even as a child she had made up stories about voyages to Djibouti, doing so with what so bordered on obsession it had caused her and Penny's parents to take her to a shrink. Though the psychiatrist had assured them there was no problem, given her "a clean bill of health," Djeannine had never forgotten the way he questioned her, the way it made her feel she had done something wrong.

This was the reason she and Penguin had not hit it off. Early in their courtship, as she more and more talked about Djibouti, Penguin had made the mistake of "interpreting" her desire to go there. Based on sound and his own thinly veiled wishes, he had said, "It means you want to be mounted from behind while being held by the waist. You want my stomach pressed against your namesake booty, my dick to part the lips of your cunt and come deep inside you." They had not, to that point, gone to bed. So blunt, so unsubtle a way of proposing that they do so meant, it turned out, they never would. Penguin had gambled, taken a chance and lost, chosen to press rather than let things take their course. He succeeded only in turning Djeannine off. She resented his bravado and

---

° None of the doors at the hotel opened or closed without creaking. Penguin saw no reason it should be any different with anagrammatic odor, synaesthetic allure.

told him so. She was deeply offended by the propositioning spin he put on Djibouti, the trivialization of her desire to go there. It took her back to her childhood, to being questioned by the shrink, the offensive assumption that her interest in Djibouti was abnormal, something which had to be interpreted, explained.

Penguin was chastened by Djeannine's rebuff. His brash proposal had surprised him even as he spoke and it shocked him more and more in retrospect as time went on. What had gotten into him he didn't know. In advancing his prepossessing "read" on Djibouti he had spoken like a man possessed, as though it were he who had been "mounted," put upon from behind, some blunt, prepossessing spirit's unwitting "horse." It had momentarily made sense at the time — a way of dispensing with courtship ritual, getting around boy/girl games, coy pretenses, getting, albeit bluntly, to the point—but Djeannine had been standoffish ever since. He now blushed whenever he thought of his indelicate "exegesis." This was the reason his tongue so unhurriedly advanced towards Penny's "cleft," the reason he forbade himself to be so bold as to call it her cunt.

Only in oblique, involuntary ways would Penny admit she had gotten Penguin on the rebound. She had seen him as a soon-to-emerge bird balled up inside a shell she grew impatient for him to crack. She had grown so impatient she mailed him the photograph of herself with the parakeet feather taped across her crotch — a way of encouraging him to "emerge" faster, come on stronger, not move so diffidently. She would never admit, even to herself, that she had sent it, though it had worked, had gotten Penguin to move more quickly and with greater assurance. Now, though, as the curtain rose on Act Two, she looked down across her chest and stomach at Penguin's head between her legs and with lids half-closed, half-open, saw it as an indistinct ball of wrinkled wings.

This was the effect of the Djibouti Eye Djeannine tele-
pathically transmitted, a soft-focus endowment which in this
particular instance rolled fledgeling flight and recuperative
bounce into one. Penny saw the entire room, not only
Penguin's head, under its auspices. Djeannine had hijacked
Penny's eyes, as it were, installing the Djibouti Eye in their
stead. It was this which made for the mist which continued to
hit like a diffuse hammer, the at-large, erotizing regard built
on contagious premises, the lack of distinct outline which
infused everything.

But the Djibouti Eye was no simple flight from sharp def-
inition, however much the soft-porn dispersal it advanced
blurred — even bordered on obliterating — the line between
this and that. The sonic apprisal of posteriority Penguin had
taken Djibouti to be was not irrelevant to the course Penny's
Djibouti-Eye-commandeered eyes now took. She let her gaze
carry past the ball of wrinkled wings between her legs and
alight upon Penguin's ass, the slow, undulatory, humping
movement of which excited her so she let out another moan.
She not only recognized but validated distinctions between
this and that. Notwithstanding the indistinct ball of wrinkled
wings his head had become, Penguin's ass was unequivocally
his ass, blunt butt. The way it moved up and down as he
humped the bed made it difficult for Penny not to grab the
ball of wrinkled wings and expedite his tongue's unhurried
progress toward her cunt. But she too was intent that, now
that their tryst at Hotel Didjeridoo was finally happening,
they both go slow, take their time.

Not unrelated to Rasta telescopy, the Djibouti Eye
advanced a Far-Eye furtherance of sight. Djibouti's proximity
to Ethiopia was lost on no one, least of all Penny. Penguin's
ass notwithstanding, she glimpsed Harrar out of one corner of
the Djibouti Eye, the Gulf of Aden out of the other. And as if

to comply with the synaesthetic premises upon which Penguin sought to establish a foothold, its infiltration of sound, scent, taste and touch added a qualitative increment to its increased reach. Penny saw, heard, smelled, tasted and felt in a single sensation under the Djibouti Eye's auspices, her commandeered eyes each occupying a separate corner while advancing a unity of image and apprehension nonetheless. Far meant miles, low notes, feel, funk and the taste on Penguin's tongue rolled into one, Harrar and the Gulf of Aden rolled in as well, Djibouti and Didjeridoo rolled in as well, ad infinitum.

Still, all was not bliss with the Djibouti Eye. Factored into the mist of which it apprised Penny was an admission that Djeannine was Penguin's lady of choice, that it was his missed opportunity with her which had brought them to Hotel Didjeridoo. The Djibouti Eye blurred the distinction between mist and "missed," belaboring with the bluntness of a hammer blow a lack so palpable missingness verged upon mystic presence. For a moment the missing lady of choice was there with such blunt subtlety it all but took Penny's breath away. The diffuse descent of Djeannine's pestering play on "missed" made her moan again.

Penguin would have been upset had he known her moans had only partly to do with him. He played the space between her legs like an instrument he thought, licking the soft insides of her thighs with all but unbearable virtuosity, all but unbearable finesse. The audible rapture into which he worked her with his tongue he heard woven in with doo-wop didjeridoo's funky-butt crescendo, the ditty-bop build-up in intensity which increasingly filled the room (an infectious mix of Mingus and Barry White, it seemed). That what he heard as funky-butt rapture was in part funky-butt despair would never have occurred to him.

By now Penny had begun to give up on getting away from Djeannine. She had suspected something was up when only a couple of days after her romance with Penguin got off the ground Djeannine announced that she was finally getting her wish, finally going to Djibouti. This was Djeannine's way, Penny had thought at the time, of upstaging her, stealing her thunder, diminishing the impact of her and Penguin hitting it off. It was her way of saying that she was unfazed (albeit the timing of the announcement said otherwise). By announcing her trip to Djibouti she insisted she had better things to think about than what her sister and a once would-be lover might be up to, that her desires and concerns were deeper than that. Djibouti bespoke longstanding sensitivity, long-lived refinement of feeling, rare depth, rare rectitude of desire.

Penny moaned in despair on realizing how tenacious Djeannine could be. The missing lady of choice's momentary presence had truly taken her aback. Rather than leaving a space in which Penguin and she could pursue their romance, Djeannine's departure had given her greater leverage, endowed her with additional power. From her vantage point in Djibouti she evidently was able to keep track of every move they made. Her ability to get inside Penny's head was a power Penny resolved to go on resisting, even though she'd begun to give up on being able to. Funky-butt rapture and funky-butt despair truly locked horns. Penny herself, out of the corner of her ear, heard it as an orchestral crescendo — dense, deeply insinuative, richly bottomed — not unlike the Aluar horn ensemble she had heard on a record of Ugandan music.

The orchestral crescendo built antithetically upon the low note's namesake root. Woven into it Penny heard a caveat, a cautionary note pitting horn against horn, yes against no. Compounded of yes as well as no, the Djibouti Eye turned inward, translating light into a high, "silent" screech played on

a newly invented horn (actually an old horn simply renamed
for the occasion), a radically antithetic horn. Funky-butt rap-
ture and funky-butt despair found themselves entwined in a
Manichean embrace, namesake root entwined with namesake
anti-root, didjeridoo entwined with didjeridon't.

Seduced by the didjeridon't's high, "silent" cry, Penny
increasingly said yes to its apparent critique of the times. She
increasingly heard it as an antidote to the widespread, facile
accent on "do" (the "_____ do it _____" bumperstickers,
"Let's do lunch sometime" and so forth). The didjeridon't's
flight from such accent she found apt and salutary.[*]

· She began to suspect that her and Penguin's tryst at Hotel
Didjeridoo had more to do with facile accent than anything
else, that they blindly obeyed the imperative "Do it," that it was
this the Djibouti Eye meant her to see. She began to envy
Djeannine's rare depth and rectitude of desire, the clean-burn-
ing flame and long-lived ardor which had taken her to Djibouti.
Compared to such lofty, longstanding passion, her and
Penguin's romance amounted to nothing, less than nothing, a
tawdry, slapdash affair. Out of the corner of her ear she could
hear she no longer moaned. She was withdrawing, increasingly
not into it, increasingly unaroused, wishing she were some-
where else. Hotel Didjeridoo had become Hotel Didjeridon't.

Penguin didn't pick up on the change in Penny's mood. He
continued addressing the beginnings of pubic hair along her
loins, letting his tongue venture a bit closer to the thick,
pungent mat and the glistening cleft underneath. This was
fortunate. It gave Penny time to recover. It amounted to an
unwitting vamp-till-ready while she gathered herself up, got

---

[*] Penny had gone to a Mingus concert in 1975. After one number, once
the applause had subsided, a man in the audience yelled out, "Yeah. Do
it, Charlie!" Mingus, annoyed, leaned over the mike and snapped,
"Do *what*, man?"

back the excitement Hotel Didjeridon't had taken away. Realizing she was falling into Djeannine's trap, that the didjeridon't was Djeannine's way of sabotaging her romance, Penny began to fight back. She resisted the Djibouti Eye's image of Djeannine's rare depth and rectitude of desire, resisted its derogation of her and Penguin's romance, turned a deaf ear to the didjeridon't.

Penny closed her eyes and immediately opened them again as wide as they would go, closed and opened them again and yet again, washing away the Djibouti Eye's influence and effect. Harrar disappeared. The Gulf of Aden disappeared. She looked down across her chest and stomach at Penguin's head between her legs. It was no longer an indistinct ball of wrinkled wings. Looking past it, she saw his ass going slowly up and down as he humped the bed.

It excited her. She felt the tip of Penguin's tongue stroke the beginnings of pubic hair along her loins. She closed her eyes, happy to be back at Hotel Didjeridoo. She moaned again. "Do it to me, Penguin, do it," she whispered as the curtain fell on Act Two.

ACT THREE

Djeannine held the empty bottle up to her left eye. She held it like a telescope, the open end to her eye, her right eye closed. The curtain had risen on Act Three after falling on the Djibouti Eye, the enabling bottle she continued to hold like a telescope, convinced its Far-Eye reach would soon return. But the bottle, for all she saw, might as well have been a penny on a dead man's eye, the patch over a pirate's eye. She stood on the dock in Djibouti facing southeast. She had lost focus, Far-Eye reach and resolution. She no longer saw all the way to Australia.

The goings-on down under had abruptly faded from view.
The ghost had gone out of the bottle, the namesake djinn
which had given Djeannine access to Penguin and Penny's
tryst at Hotel Didjeridoo. She now waited and waited and
waited, not ready to believe the telepathic telescopy she'd
been granted would not soon be restored. She held the bottle
up to her eye, straining to see what Penguin and Penny were
up to, thwarted by the see-thru spirit's departure, the pirate's-
patch blackness it had left behind. She was insistent it come
back, incensed it would dare to leave, convinced will and
resolve were all it would take. She learned otherwise.

Djeannine stood and stood and stood, waiting for the
Djibouti Eyes's return, waiting for the namesake djinn, the
see-thru spirit, to inhabit the bottle again. She continued
holding the bottle up to her eye, turning it from time to time
as if to focus it, switching it from eye to eye every so often —
all to no avail. Will and resolve, she began to see, were not the
same as Far-Eye reach and resolution. Her indignation began
to subside, give way to acceptance. The goings-on at Hotel
Didjeridoo were off-screen, no longer accessible to the talis-
manic bottle she held in her hands. This was the sad, accept-
ing realization which moved her to lower the bottle from her
eye and to stand, hands at her side, the bottle in her right
hand, resignedly staring out across the water. She stood that
way for what seemed like eternity though it was only a couple
of minutes at most.

She raised the bottle to her lower lip and began to blow
across the opening. What moved her to do this was the same
sad, accepting realization, only infinitely more mature now
owing to eternity's two-minute stay. The sound she made was
likewise infinitely mature, as though it had lain within the bot-
tle for aeons, all of time — rich, dark, resonant, mellow
beyond belief. It was a sound which bestowed a blessing and

a kiss. She blew for every wish which had never been granted, letting all the tense will and resolve go out with each breath.

Djeannine blew without knowing the ghost had returned to the bottle. She had no way of knowing the namesake djinn which had gone away had now come back. No longer the avatar of ocular access it had been before, it endowed the bottle with rare audiotactile reach. She felt a buzz where her bottom lip pressed against the bottle's rim, as though an invisible reed vibrated against it with the rapidity of a hummingbird's wing. She was unable to know it was the see-thru spirit's return in another form, its translation of ocular access into synaesthetic hum. She was equally unable to know that the namesake djinn whose names were legion (Jarred Bottle, Flaunted Fifth, DB, Djbot Baghostus. . .) had now taken a new one, Djbouche. With increasingly caressive insistence, her embouchure altered so as to elicit pitch variations. Djbouche endowed the normally monotone bottle with the ability to render a tune. The tune Djeannine now began to play was "I Cover the Waterfront."

She gave it all she had, more than she had. She hummed as she blew across the opening, à la Yusef Lateef or Rahsaan Roland Kirk, hummed and played the tune at the same time. It was a technique she had seen called *zemzemeh* on an album of music from Luristan in Iran, a technique resorted to by a nay-player accompanying a song whose lyrics complained of "the taste of separation." This was indeed the audiotactile "taste" in Djeannine's mouth, the synaesthetic lament for lost ocular access to the off-screen goings-on at Hotel Didjeridoo. Djeannine covered the waterfront, lamenting the loss not of love but of power, not "in search of my love," as the lyrics insist, but in resigned acceptance of the Djibouti Eye's eclipse. The "desolate docks" on which she stood were desolate not because of "the one I love" having gone away. "Will you return?" was the rhetorical question she asked not of "my love" but of the Far-Eye reach and resolution she had been so abruptly separated from.

Djeannine had no way of knowing how much in touch with Hotel Didjeridoo she continued to be. Penguin noticed, at that very moment, a warm gust of wind caress the small of his back, a warm gust which brushed his skin like an ostrich feather. The blown-bottle effect of the low flute which had just entered the music piped into the room also did not escape his notice. It was an alto or a bass flute — he wasn't sure which—and it lent itself to doo-wop didjeridoo's initiatic riff. The warm gust blew over the small of his back and across his buttocks as he continued slowly humping the bed. His rump's antiphonal rise and fall soon obeyed a rhythm introduced by Djbouche, an onomatopoetic meeting of oomph and whoosh the low flute had become the exponent of.

Penny, whose eyes were still closed, also felt a warm gust of wind. It blew across her face and, as with Penguin, it felt like an ostrich feather brushing her skin. Even so, Djeannine didn't cross her mind. The contact was infinitely more subtle than the Djibouti Eye's intrusion. She felt the warm gust brush her face and she also heard the low flute's blown-bottle accent. It had a way of etherealizing the funky-butt rush woven into the music piped into the room. The way it had had its way with her, seized her, sent a shiver running down her back.

Djeannine, still standing on the dock in Djibouti, continued to blow with unwitting reach. Djbouche, unbeknown to her, had long since bid the Djibouti Eye goodbye, long since acceded to the throne emptied by its ouster. Djeannine blew across the bottle's opening, knowing it was an empty socket she blew across, knowing it more than she knew. Djbouche bore the knowing she kept from herself, a way she'd had with knowing—wanting but not wanting to know—ever since she was a child. Djibouti had been the elsewhere knowing would not reach, but now that she was there Hotel Didjeridoo took its place. The off-screen goings-on between Penguin and Penny she both knew and wanted not to know, knew and wanted not to see. She wanted to know and not know, wanted to know and not see, "know" both bound up with and unbound by "see." This was the mixed benediction (blessing and kiss, blessing and curse) borne by Djbouche, oomph woven in with whoosh by their meeting's low logarithmic flute.

Djeannine extracted more music from "I Cover the Waterfront" than anyone ever had. It was all the more miraculous that she did it on a normally monotone bottle. The bottle itself was the "desolate dock" spoken of in the song. Djeannine played upon and made a music of its emptiness, its evacuation by the Djibouti Eye. Vacuity was the voided ground she stood upon, the hollow premises upon which oomph and whoosh rested and relied. Dearth and desolation so eloquently spoke at Djbouche's behest it would have been all anyone within earshot could have done not to burst into tears. There was no one within earshot however. Djeannine stood all alone on the dock.

Djeannine's "I Cover the Waterfront" acknowledged Billie Holiday's version, but only to go on to surpass it. Acknowledgement took the form of an insinuative accent, à la Billie, on the first syllable of the word *cover*. That she blew across a lack of cover came into dialectical play with the very accent she advanced. The bottle got the sound of a gasba, the Arabico-Berber flute, scattered breath suggesting wasted breath, leakage, loss. Djbouche was the genie let out of the lamp, wasted wish as well as wasted breath, an abrasive wind intent on scouring the air. There was no cover, no place to hide, it seemed to insist. The "desolate dock" across which she blew confirmed the "desolate dock" upon which she stood, an abject, abandoned waterfront which offered no cover.

The blown bottle's abrasive wind advanced an audiotactile equivalent of the grainy telescopy which filled Penny and Penguin's room. It was the audible counterpart of the soft-focus mist the Djibouti Eye brought on, the blows of a diffuse hammer translated into sound. It was a warm desert wind. It was a weird, resistant wind, the weirdest wind which had ever blown. Insinuative accent found itself entwined with lost access, a lament for lost ocular access embroidered by the reach of an erotizing foray. It was a wind whose elegiac embrace blew without respite, desolate wind woven in with desolate waterfront, blown blessing and kiss rolled into one.

Djeannine sought refuge, cover, consolation in the bottle she blew. She had begun to blow when telepathic access turned against her, when ocular access turned aural, when something she heard put her on the defensive. Not long after the goings-on down under had gone off-screen Djeannine had become prey to an alternate transmission. As she stood on the dock holding the bottle at her side, resignedly accepting the Djibouti Eye's eclipse, she had begun to hear what she no longer saw, the goings-on at Hotel Didjeridoo. She heard Penny's moans, heard heavy breathing, heard her whisper, "Do it to me, Penguin, do it," over and over again. It was as if she had become the receiver, Penny the transmitter. It was as if the Djibouti Eye had not simply closed but had boomeranged against her, undergoing a synaesthetic transla-tion on its return. It struck her with the force of an obscene telephone call. It was partly due to this that she had raised the bottle to her mouth and begun to blow. It was partly a way of covering her ears.

Djeannine filled the air with a spray of sound. In part she blew to drown out Penny's "Do it to me, Penguin, do it," to drown out the noise from down under, turn a deaf ear to Penny's pantings and moans. She blew loud, but with no loss of nuance, no collapse of what she played into mere oomph. Djbouche, unbeknown to her, was in the bottle. She blew, not knowing how far.

Off-screen, Penny grew more and more impatient, less and less able to resist expediting Penguin's unhurried progress toward the cleft between her legs. The warm wind continued to blow across her face, an ostrich feather fanning the flames.

Unbeknown to Penny, Penguin grew more impatient as well. A warm wind continued to blow across the small of his back and across his buttocks, insistent he not take so much time, it seemed to him. He resisted, letting his tongue linger as unhurriedly as ever upon the beginnings of pubic hair along her loins. He was relieved, however, when Penny, unable to wait any longer, took hold of the back of his head and gently pulled, causing his mouth to fill with hair, his tongue to part the salty-sweet lips underneath.

Penny, feeling the warmth and the wetness of Penguin's mouth, emitted a mix of moan and sigh, ecstasy and relief. Djeannine blew that much louder as the curtain fell on Act Three.

Dear Angel of Dust,

Once again I'm writing while convalescing in bed —
another round of shattered cowrie shell attacks, shattered-
shell-become-buzzing-bottle-cap attacks. My head feels like a
calabash wrapped around an mbira. I hear the plucking of
metal keys, a slow, methodical plucking which sounds like a
leaky faucet at first, then builds and becomes more compli-
cated over time. It's as though the drops of water aren't con-
tent simply to drop and go down the drain or to drip and be
absorbed in the cup or whatever it is of water they fall into.
They insist on living beyond their descent, dancing rather
than disappearing, kept alive by cross-accentual ricochet and
recurrence.

How much this has to do with Hotel Didjeridoo I can't say.
A good deal it would seem, as it's neither Ornette's
"Embraceable You" nor Lightnin's "Bottle Up and Go" but
"Drennethology," Penguin's piece, I hear piped into my head.
An imagino-cathartic edifice built on "Drennethology's" how-
high harmonics (Drennette says jump, Penguin asks how
high) is what my head seems to have become. Call it a carni-
val hive, a Junkanoo house worn on my head which *is* my
head, a house built in resonant rapport with wouldly reach
(wouldly fall as well as wouldly rise). Call it Hotel Didjeridoo
if you like, but it's really less a wind axe than a plucked one—
Hotel Mbira or, in its lowest wouldly register, Hotel Bagana.
At moments of lowest wouldly descent my head is a trape-
zoidal wooden frame with a skin-covered soundbox at the
smaller end, a Davidic harp strung with strings made of sheep
gut. U-shaped leather thong buzzers amplify the sound. At
such moments my head is nothing if not a hotel, home away

from home, an exilic harp, diasporic play upon exile, pitched,
like a tent, in transit, peripatetic, plucked. Still, I can't help
wondering how home can be away from home. How can
home so divide itself as to be other than itself, severed, self-
same, either/and all at once? How can home be in more than
one place at the same time?

Yet "home away from home" so succinctly says it I don't
know why I go on so. It's clearly an aspect of my condition to
go on so. "Home away from home" titrates the entrance and
the reintroduction (woof to "Drennethology's" warp) of an
mbira piece whose title, "Nhemamusasa," means "The
Cutting of Branches for a Temporary Shelter." Nominal hotel
notwithstanding, music as movement thru a makeshift suc-
cession of huts calibrates while conducing diasporic drift.
Each plucked key proffers makeshift shelter, ephemeral
"structure" on the order of a shantytown lean-to, exactly the
tentlike shelter made of branches the Shona mean by *musasa*.
Call it Hotel Musasa-Turned-Junkanoo-Headdress. A succes-
sion of huts-worn-atop-the-head file thru my head, a
Junkanoo parade, a procession of heads within my head, huts
within the hut my head thus becomes. No elaborate house, no
stately mansion, my head becomes a warrior's hut, makeshift
shelter made of branches on a march into the bush. Call it
rickety weave equilibrating "domicility" with romp. Home
away from home, in short. Everyone tells me it's all in my
head. Moot solace. The problem is that it *is* in my head.

It all came about, this latest round of attacks, yesterday at
rehearsal. Lambert suggested we work an early Shepp tune
into our book, a tune Shepp recorded with the New York
Contemporary Five, "Like A Blessed Baby Lamb." It's a tune
no one plays anymore, not even Shepp himself, but it's a tune
it took none of us much time to recall. "Oh yeah, I remember
that one," Aunt Nancy was the first to say. It's a tune whose

infectious head had stayed with all of us over the years,
though none of us, other than Lambert, had heard it or given
it much thought for quite some time. Advancing a mix of
croaked insistence and wry wager, it's a tune whose infectious
head all the more infectiously tapers — tapers to assume the
contour of an acquiescent growl, a wistful growl. It's a tune we
quickly agreed to have a go at.

The namesake aspect of Lambert's suggestion soon made
itself clear, so clear it became hard to believe we hadn't seen
it right away. Following a couple of aborted starts, we hit on
our third try, Drennette and Aunt Nancy laying down the
rhythm as straightforwardly as one could want. Drennette
kept straightahead time on the cymbal while Aunt Nancy, on
bass, walked as if her life, if not all our lives, depended on it.
Still, this didn't preclude the introduction of a hesitant or a
hasty step every now and then, a fearful, fugitive tread which
proved to be the base Lambert built his namesake solo on.

I say namesake solo because after only two or three bars
that was clearly what it was. It was clear Lambert took the
tune's title to heart, however much he complicated nominal
meekness, lamblike meekness, with under-the-breath invec-
tive, namesake beatitude, namesake boast. Which is to say
that while *lamb* was clearly the facet on which his accent fell,
ram inflected that accent with under-the-breath bluster, gruff
pronouncement, self-praise. The horn's gruff, sandpaper
tonalities abraded namesake meekness even as Lambert
extolled his lamblike virtues. He resorted to a taut, semisung,
semiswallowed moan which was a muffled moan, a moan
smothered in lamb's wool, it seemed. So seeming, it made it
clear Lambert thereby renamed or nicknamed himself Lamb,
recalling the night Djamilaa soothed and consoled Penguin,
calling him Pen. He too wished to be babied, consoled,
addressed by a motherly voice, a wish Djamilaa took little

time to grant him, interjecting a wordless, lullabylike run which put one in mind of a Wagogo soothing song.

Lambert called out to be consoled, however, only to fly from such announcement of need, to flee whatever answering embrace might be forthcoming. In doing so he renamed or nicknamed himself Lam, nicked his name further. This he did by availing himself of the opening advanced by Drennette and Aunt Nancy's fugitive tread — rhythmic permission on which he built the namesake bifurcation he sounded again and again. Fugitive tread's divergence from straightahead lope underwrote Lam's analogous divergence from Lamb. Lamb bleated, cooed, cried, poignantly pleaded for care and understanding. Lam, on the other hand, darted, dashed as though driven, daunted all hope of straightforward access or capture, emotional and otherwise.

It was a devastating one-two punch, Lam in more senses than one. It was all I could do to keep my head on straight, actually more than I could do to keep my head on straight, taken out as I was by Lambert's Lamb/Lam combination. Lamb/Lam, that is, exacted a vibratory tension, so tautly rolling pulse into one with punch as to become corpuscular (part airy, openhanded slap, part haymaker fist).

Not only did I feel I'd been hit upside the head but I understood "upside" in a new epistemic light, saw how deeply, how resonantly, "upside" said it all. "Upside" spoke for angularity, glancing access. More locus than location, "upside" spoke for tendency, tangency, the tease of a play on intangibility, oblique — not straightforwardly inside or outside, not straightforwardly both. No wonder huts-worn-atop-the-head file thru my head. Tenancy, interiority, what was housed, had now to be understood as itineracy, Lamb/Lam's tangential address.

No wonder strings made of sheep gut vibrated. No wonder cowrie-shells-turned-into-bottle-caps buzzed and have gone

on buzzing. Threaded in with everything else —
"Drennethology," "Nhemamusasa," Junkanoo drums, exilic
harp — I still hear Lam telling Lamb to come off it, Lamb
purveying its theme of needy innocence nonetheless.

                         Yours,
                           N.

Dear Angel of Dust,

Yesterday as I lay in bed convalescing from the latest bottle cap attacks I heard the sound of something hitting my bedroom window. It sounded as if someone were tossing pebbles at the window, though the sound, a tapping sound, seemed of something lighter and less compact than pebbles, not so solid a sound, a tinnier sound. I didn't pay it much mind at first, not at all sure it wasn't simply a new thread in the cross-accentual cloth my head had become, but after a while I could clearly tell it was coming from outside rather than inside my head. It was clearly the sound of something hitting the window pane. After a dozen or so taps I got up and went to the window to see what was up. I looked out the window and what I saw, about fifteen feet away, was Djamilaa, feet planted firmly on the ground, arched back like a limbo dancer, holding a bottle cap between the middle finger and thumb of her right hand, just behind her shoulder at about the level of her ear. With a flick of her middle finger, a snap, she sent the bottle cap flying, arcing thru the air toward the window. It hit the window with a tap, clearly and exactly the sound I'd been hearing. I looked down at the ground just below the window, where the bottle cap fell, and saw what I already knew, that it wasn't the first.

There were bottle caps which had already been launched lying on the ground just below the window. There were even more which were yet to be launched lying in a paper bag sitting on the ground to Djamilaa's right. No sooner did she launch one than she reached into the bag and took out another. She launched them one right after another, nonstop, shooting them high into the air so that they hit the window on their way down. They spun like tiny flying saucers, cutting a high, hyper-

bolic arc thru the air. The play of arcs — her body's backward-
bending arc and the bottle caps' high, sun-seeking arc — bor-
dered on sublime. I stood at the window transfixed, entranced.
Her body seemed a bow, each bottle cap an arrow. I stood cap-
tivated by her body's bowlike bottle cap launch. Her backward
bend seemed an obverse evocation of early Egyptian sky, taut
bow and heavenly bend rolled into one, albeit obverse bow.
Her thin body's limbo harmonics not only brought arc into play
with arc, how-low into play with how-high, but bow (bo) into
play with bow (bau), inverse bow (bau).

Rolling arrow and flying saucer into one, each bottle cap's
quantum coalescence effected a head-on, bull's-eye hit and a
glancing blow. This, I soon saw, was Djamilaa's answer to the
shattered cowrie shell attack, the shattered-shell-turned-bot-
tle-cap attack, her counterattack. Each bottle cap, as it hit the
window and fell to the ground, tugged at and seemed to take
with it some of the tension which filled my head, the com-
pacted, full-to-bursting feeling the attacks entail. It was as if
my skull relaxed, emitted a subtle sigh of relief, as each bot-
tle cap fell to the ground. Djamilaa seemed to be saying that
ridding me of the attack was a snap, child's play, as elementary
as the game of shooting bottle caps we played as kids.

It went farther than that however. I stared out the window
at Djamilaa, entranced by the sculpted grace of her arced
body, the way the light cotton dress she wore draped her
midriff and thighs. She showed no sign of having noticed me
standing there. She too seemed entranced, caught up in the
methodical rhythm of shooting bottle caps one after another.
Over time she bent farther and farther back, arcing the bottle
caps higher and higher. These were the sublimest bottle cap
flights I had ever seen. I'd have hoped in vain, I'm sure, had
I hoped to see any more sublime. Each bottle cap, at the apex
of its arc, seemed to rival the sun, to compete with the sun for

suzerainty over an otherwise unlit world. So bright was arced ascendancy it forced me to close my eyes.

Upon closing my eyes I saw myself seated in a bottle cap which had been turned upside down. Whether it was that the bottle cap had grown or that I had shrunk I wasn't sure, but I clearly saw myself seated inside it as it spun. It reminded me of the teacup ride at Disneyland. The bottle cap spun and spun and spun, spinning me with it, so fast I had to hold on to its edge to keep from flying out. It spun thru soundless, oddly unlit space (bottle cap suzerainty, bottle cap eclipse), though the lack of light had no effect on my ability to see. The sound-lessness — a malarial deafness it seemed — had more impact on me, a veritable dream of suppressed resonance, older than rhythm, even older than time. I hungered after sound so rav-enously I opened my eyes again, hoping to again hear the sound of bottle caps hitting the window.

My eyes were open only long enough to see how dizzy I was. The room — the whole world in fact — was spinning. I immediately lost my legs and fell to the floor, blacking out on my way down. The next thing I knew I was coming to, lying on my back looking up at Djamilaa, who was kneeling over me shaking me gently, bringing me back. I instinctively went to shake my head to clear it of cobwebs, only to find I didn't need to, that it was the clearest it had been in days — no "Nhemamusasa," no Hotel Bagana, no Junkanoo-huts-worn-atop-the-head and so forth. Djamilaa smiled at the look of surprise on my face. My head's been clear ever since.

As ever,

N.

Dear Angel of Dust,

What a relief getting out to play can be. I don't subscribe to the putting down of "head trips" (headiness appeals to me as much for its inner as its outer dispatch) but there's something to be said for the notion that you can dwell too long or too much in your own head. The gig we just got back from, three nights in San Francisco at Keystone Korner, makes me think it's this my recent bottle cap attacks were about. It was as if I'd been let out of some place I'd been cooped up in for too long. Djamilaa's curative bottle cap launches notwithstanding, my head had remained more tight than I realized, more subtly compacted thanks to Djamilaa's intervention but compacted still. It was as if getting away for the gig in San Francisco let out what subtle pressure persisted (like letting air out of a balloon one thought was empty). It relieved me of the bottle caps' lingering impact, apprising me of it as it also rid me of it, an all but audible "hiss" announcing bottle cap residuum's heady retreat.

No doubt it was good to get out of town as well. The smog's always worse come summer, which with the heat makes outside so uninviting I tend to pull in—perhaps too far in. In any case, I felt a further release of pressure as we travelled north. Bottle cap impactedness, albeit by now all the more subtle, let up the farther away we got from L.A. Indeed, so subtle did its grip become that it got harder to tell whether it let up or simply held on with greater finesse. It was the lightest touch (if it was a touch) I'd ever felt—so light it seemed to have become light itself by the time we rolled past San Miguel. Bottle cap finesse now so seamlessly sewed touch and intangibility together that the osmotic exchange between inside and out made it feel as if my forehead—all and/or nothing at all—was no longer there, not only the all which wasn't all there but also the nothing which almost was. For a moment I was indeed light-headed in the most fleet, far-reaching sense — a fleet sense which never entirely went away I would later find out.

None of this is to say that outside lost any of the grounded spin which makes it a world. Nor was the gruff interiority of which the shattered cowrie shell and/or bottle cap attacks are an outward sign at all relinquished by bottle cap finesse's furtive stitch. Part cough, part call to prayer, gruff interiority infused earth and sky with an animate glint which appeared to scour them from within. Scoured earth and sky cried out for bottle cap finesse's reconnoitering spin, an umbilical aubade which bid aliquant ambush goodbye, the closest inside and out would ever come to adequation. What was in was also out not so much in that to be either was to be both as in that spin locked arms with spin as in a dance, an embrace whose wrought elasticity made waves, a gruff, corded quiver running back and forth. The brown, undulant hills to the east were such waves, reconnoitering roll made malleable, palpable, possessed. One needed only to reach out the window and grab hold.

Mile after mile went by with those hills to our right. They had the look of sanded wood at times, an elision of crevice and curvature so adroit they appeared to have been molded by a sculptor's hands. At times they had the look of limbless torsos, recumbent flesh coaxed into an obdurate mix of art and unselfconsciousness. It was the grace of that condition or conditionlessness one was tempted to reach out the window and grab, convinced one could reach out and grab, so fleet had in's reconnoitering traverse of out now become, so stolid out's apparent habitation of in. Mound after mound rose and fell, spread and flowed, one into another, the comeliest cali-

bration of rise and recline I've ever seen. Sunlight hit the
browned grass they were covered with at just the right angle
(it was late afternoon) and made it look as though the hills,
like "frosted" lightbulbs, were aglow with their own inner
light, muted light. Such light was in fact the synaesthetic vari-
able advancing an equation of sight with sound, a low-key,
subterranean hum which was otherwise mute. Strings had
been buried underground it seemed, plucked guts parlayed
into polyvocalic root, chthonic strum. We all sat in silence
looking out the windows as the brown rolling hills promised
to go on forever and we ourselves rolled on past San Lucas,
King City, Salinas. . .

   An aura lay about the hills. It clung without actually touch-
ing them, a heaving, low-to-the-ground cover not unlike fog,
except that it aided rather than obstructed the eye. One saw
what one would otherwise not have seen, the topographic
spread if not spillage of a "frosted" effect, summer sun and
the hills' torsolike allure notwithstanding. Indeed, such effect
abetted every bodily hint the hills possessed, each erogenous
crevice, curve and rumpish roll all the more insistent under
the soft-focus look it bestowed. The browned grass was an
extensive body hair the angular sun lent a matte, oddly lunar
light, halo and haunt so deftly rolled into one that the hills
were no less ablaze for being "frosted," no less lyric albeit
mute. We sat, looked and listened, rolling along, subterranean
strum an immaterial web tying us to our seats.

   I looked at Djamilaa sitting next to me out of the corner of
my eye and I could see that she saw and heard what I saw and
heard. Out of the same corner I looked around the van and
saw that Drennette, Lambert, Aunt Nancy and Penguin saw
and heard it too. This turned out to be a tuning up of sorts and
a sound check of sorts, not only previous to those we later did
at the club but ontically prior, proto-, fundamental albeit dif-

fuse. There wasn't a note we played during the whole gig which wasn't inflected by subterranean strum, our proto-tune-up-and-sound-check-rolled-into-one's chthonic stir. Having sat, looked and listened for so long, having been so enthralled, we exacted a rolling contour from the music we must've long suspected was there but never so explicitly actualized until this gig. Contour and contagion met one another unawares it appeared, so instinctively threaded, so hypnotically stitched was the cloth we donned, a cloak of sound which heaved and throbbed like involuntary tissue, a living organ.

We were, in that regard, "live at Keystone Korner" in more senses than one. This in fact made for difficulties during the sound check we did once we got to the club. The music, albeit peppered with glottal reports whose flayed cut and cutaneous flap were anything but soporific, had a steadying effect on the sound engineer, induced an awake but oddly adjunct state, a sort of waking sleep. He drifted in and out, his attention not always where it should've been, and getting the levels right, the mix right, the placement of the mikes right and so forth took a lot more time than it normally would've. Over and over one of us had to leave the stage and walk back to the sound booth to rouse him from his rapt adjacency. He apologized each time, saying he was normally much more efficient, asking us to bear with him, mumbling with increasing wonder something about the music's adjunct address.

Were I to say that out followed us in I'd be telling only part of it. Rumpish roll acquired an introspective quiver, a mind-itch deeply enough interred to invest all premises, the club's, not surprisingly, prime among those it endowed on this particular occasion. Cutaneous flap was our attempt at "answering" not only subterranean strum but subcortical irritant, though this turned out, in the sound man's case, to have a different effect. Subcortical irritant, not so much "answered" as accelerated until we got the right mix, invited secretions of adjunct rapture, rapt adjacency's eventual pearl, "answering" pearl. This, at any rate, was the sense I had of it, given that once we got the levels where we wanted them rapt adjacency no longer took the sound man out. Looked at accordingly, in, in the person of the sound man, could be said to have followed us out up until that point. Whatever the case, the story I mean to tell isn't so much that one as another one, that of our first public performance of "Like A Blessed Baby Lamb," an impromptu debut which bears upon what I began this letter talking about — bottle cap finesse's furtive stitch, fugitive stitch.

It was during the first night of the gig, the end of it in fact. All had gone well, exceptionally well, and the audience, at the end of the second set, rose from their seats and insisted on an encore. I was the one who suggested we encore with "Like A Blessed Baby Lamb." It was a throwing down of a gauntlet of sorts, a test and a dare, my resolve to see how far bottle cap impactedness had pulled back, how real its retreat in fact was. My head was light, a see-thru amenity, weightless, but I wondered would it remain so under the brunt of "upside" itineracy, Lamb/Lam's tangential address.

"Why not?" Drennette was quick to say—quick as well to count off the time while tapping it out on the ride cymbal. We were into it before we knew it.

A ride it very much turned out to be, notwithstanding the slow, almost dirgelike pace Drennette meted out. It seemed we dredged whatever ground it was we traversed as we began, as if to unearth the umbilical quiver subterranean strum so insisted on. The accordingly "collapsed" contour of the piece, the staggered eloquence within the ruin of prepossessing traipse it apprised one of, came into arch, enabling play with reconnoitering roll. Lambert put a pestering spin on Shepp's

allusion to a train whistle's moan, a frayed lowing which con-
jured smoke seen receding from afar. The brown rolling hills
we'd earlier driven past grew possessed of trails of locomotive
smoke, as did the sense of topographic spread the Websterian
buzz Lambert resorted to evoked. Topographic spread served
a corollary sense of tautologic inclusion while antiphonal
qualm and/or qualification brought the other horns in.
Penguin, Djamilaa and I formed a tricorn chorus (he on alto,
she and I on trumpets) which amended Lambert's gruff semi-
otic smoke while exhorting him all the more. Lambert blew
smoke and we answered with a swart, sway figure, all on
behalf of tautologic totality, tautologic inclusion — he as if to
say, "Everything is everything," we as if to say, "Except when
it's not." We coaxed and called his bluff at the same time.

"So far so good," I said to myself several bars into the
piece, relieved to find my head still unimpacted, unimpaired
by "upside" itineracy, though I knew the tough parts were yet
to come. Lambert's bluster came into pestering play with
nominal meekness, possessed of a ramlike, trainlike power,
Lamb notwithstanding, possessed of a leonine ferocity as
well. Lamb's wool, ram's horn, train whistle's moan and lion's
roar indeed all stood as one, an upstart amalgam only
"upside" itineracy could've concocted, but my head's unim-
pacted amenity held its own. The apparent "pauses to reflect"
written into the piece no doubt helped — not only the
backpedaling figure our tricorn chorus offered up, but also
the slight, strategic rest right before the paradelike passage,
the parade-turning-into-car-truck-and-bus-horns-in-mid-
Manhattan-traffic passage.

The real test, I knew, would be Lambert's solo coming out
of that passage. Indeed, he was on it from note one, inviting
any and all who would to rethink the paradelike swell which
had gone before. He bellowed, to begin, as if mired in tar, a

pestered, put-upon sound evoking prehistoric animals going under in pits, a thick sludge of a sound which unpaved and undermined the paradelike premises on which we'd stood only moments before. Impediment (senses of problematic tread) vied with implied advance, parade elation. Paradelike premises were now decidedly left behind but only partially put away, as the very hope of parade advance turned into spectre, a deferred ghost haunting the hope it otherwise instilled or insisted on. Lambert evidently felt such insistence as prod, prepossessing lope, for he gradually quickened the pace, tar pit premises notwithstanding, sludge notwithstanding, pulling Drennette and Aunt Nancy along. What better reason to run than tar pit premises' rained-on parade, the sense of being stuck, he implicitly asked.

Still, it was anything but an out and out run—less that than a sense of tenuous hold he applied to each note, as if the sound, even the horn itself, were on the verge of getting away. He blew as though he fought to keep up or to catch up. The getaway twist he gave each note was retrospectively the spur which appeared to quicken the pace. Thus, it only seemed he pulled Drennette and Aunt Nancy along. That he effected an appearance of tempo change through ambiguations of pitch, the burred expanse of a note confounding lag with lurch, is a fact which, hard if not impossible to give an account of, there's nonetheless a name for: Lam. It was a beautiful, brilliant move on Lambert's part, given that the overblown, bellowing tack with which he'd set out thereby showed or punningly implied itself to've been an overstated version of Lamb, bellow an overblown version of bleat, prehistoric bleat. The getaway twist he increasingly gave each note not only fled or attempted to flee tar pit premises but tended, more specifically, toward Lamb, stole away to Lamb, again, albeit differently, rolling Lam and Lamb into one.

The sense of strata which both distinguished and linked bellow and bleat, tar pit and pavement, was a new wrinkle no doubt introduced by chthonic strum. Tar pit premises notwithstanding, Aunt Nancy's walking bass was as steady as ever, an assured, insistent tread Lambert chose to take issue with now and again, interjecting reminders of tar pit ordeal, tar pit duress. In so doing, he brought Lam's other side or sense into play, a pugilistic refusal to abide by the bedrock amenities he otherwise invited, a bellowing bone Lam picked with Lamb's wish to be cradled, reassured. Such reassurance came under loud indictment, steal-away wish and intrepid cradle rocked as one albeit kept at a distance, a split, spitting figure Lambert came back to more than once. It was all he could do to contain Lam's bluster, equally all he could do to keep Lamb's bleat from becoming maudlin, melodramatic.

There were two things Lamb/Lam seemed intent on saying. "I'm rough and I'm tough and I don't take no stuff" was Lam's unabashed boast, the gruff bravado which made for a mix with Lamb's low-key disquiet, Lamb's lament that (this was the second thing) we had yet to advance beyond muck, prehistoric mire. Indeed, Lamb, the ostensible baby (namesake baby), came right out and called itself Tar Baby, making explicit what up until then had only been implied. Lam's punches held him (Lam) captive, getaway twist or steal-away wish notwithstanding, Lamb's low-key self-nomination announced.

It was an idea which Penguin, Djamilaa and I ratified at once, offering up an impromptu unison figure whose "we-hear-you" inflection put the finishing touch on Lambert's split, spitting mien or motif. Yes, better to think of history as not yet begun, better to insist on some future inception, that what had passed and continued to pass for it wasn't where we were headed, that the true advent of humanity lay ahead —

this was the responsive chord Lambert had touched and with which we now replied. As low-key as Lamb's disquiet, we comprised a sedate chorus, a chaste, oddly sibylline amen corner, dispensing our repeated "we-hear-you" with utmost composure, utmost calm. Lam, on the other hand, thrashed and bellowed boast after boast, spouting threats and spitting out curses, thickening the tar pit preserve its attempt to punch its way out of only made worse, prehistoric premises Lamb would've helped it flee had it only been able.

But so low-key was Lamb's disquiet one wondered at points was Lamb really there. Was its presence no more than promised or implied, a homonymic "twin," semantic twist or detour notwithstanding, conjured by Lam, contrapuntally conjured or constituted, an eponymic arrival ever to arise in the nick of time, the very nick out of which Lam itself had arisen and repeatedly arose? Lambert blew this and other questions our way, more and more insisting we no longer resort to such easy response as our repeated "we-hear-you," upping the ante on post-prehistoric Lamb, presumed human advent.

By now we were well into Lambert's solo and still my head's unimpacted amenity remained intact. Not even the hint of a bottle cap buzz arose to distract me, much less a parade of Junkanoo huts. "Drennethology," "Nhemamusasa," exilic harp and all couldn't have been farther away. Some other world it seemed they were part of when, for one moment, I gave them any thought at all. No, the gauntlet had clearly been thrown down and clearly bottle cap impactedness remained in retreat.

This continued to be the case despite Lam/Lamb's vibratory harmonics growing more and more fierce. Lambert increasingly let us know that unison assent wasn't good enough, that no sedate chorus, no chaste amen corner, came close to being adequate to the task his bleat-within-bellow hopefully prompted or at least proposed. Something more strained or strung out seemed to be in order. Lambert's split, spitting fierceness and fury grew even more split, more splintered, more ferocious, moving Penguin, Djamilaa and me to adopt a split, splintered approach of our own. Unison assent gave way to a staggered, scattered, catch-as-catch-can fray in the fabric which up until then we'd so sedately woven.

Djamilaa was the first to diverge, taking the trumpet from her lips and singing the wordless, lullabylike motif which recalled a Wagogo soothing song. She sought, it seemed, to caress the disconsolate Lamb/Lam rift away, kiss it with a mother's medicinal kiss, make it all better. Penguin, less than a beat behind, darted off in a different direction, concocting a high run of bittersweet flutter, bird-wing flash, making light of Lambert's tar pit complaint. I let a beat and a half go by before joining in with a split, spitting rush of wind which was all the more spitting and split for being played on trumpet, thereby beating Lambert at his own game or at least aiming to. Our unison assent's uniform fabric was now multiply inflected, multiply frayed, multiply worn if not outright rent, a thin, threadbare cloth caroling dredge and redress. It all made for a wild witches' brew of a sound which was not uninformed by subterranean strum. Subterranean strum, that is, added further undertones of tear, seismic tatter, chthonic rent. Dues went deeper than we thought it seemed to say.

Lambert's was no longer the dominant voice. We were now into a collectively improvised passage, a cacophonous bridge which was what he'd had in mind when he began to poohpooh our unison assent. He let his tenor fade a bit, fall into the fray, not so much resolving Lamb/Lam's dialectics as letting it dissolve, one voice, albeit splintered, split, among several. Lambert refused to disentangle Lamb and Lam but instead let their adhesion infuse the bridge or brew we were concocting, a bridge or brew from which or out of which one of us, we knew, would soon get the nod to launch his or her solo. That nod, when it came, came my way, not exactly catching me unprepared but, even so, caught up in recollecting Djamilaa's bottle cap launching bend. That bend, not our cacophonous brew, was the bridge I would cross or which would carry me across I couldn't help feeling — a feeling which made me pause, ever so slightly hesitate before launching my solo.

As it turned out, I knew more than I knew, for Djamilaa did indeed play a peculiar role in my solo, though not a role involving her bottle cap launching bend in any literal way. It would be safe to say, however, that a certain articulacy came into my playing, an advanced ability to bend notes I don't normally have when I play trumpet, an ability bestowed by my reflecting on her bottle cap launching bend if not by the bend itself. "Stay loose" was the implied advice it gave and this I did, but its impact and/or instruction went much farther than that.

I began with a dilated, hemorrhaging sound, advancing the Lamb aspect of Lambert's solo to insist that brass had something to do with blood, that to bleat was to bleed. Brass Lamb tinctured seepages of widening alarm, bleeding mainly air, titrating the mix whereby what brass had to do with blood gained atmospheric effect. It was a big, epochal sound it seemed — pressured, apocalyptic, as intimate as gossip nonetheless. I stayed loose, holding bottle cap impactedness at bay, doing so without giving it a thought.

Although Penguin and Lambert took their horns from their mouths once I got going, Djamilaa continued singing the wordless, Wagogo-like air she'd woven into the frayed, cacophonous bridge we crossed. This no doubt made it easier to keep bottle cap impactedness at bay, though there's reason to believe it stayed away of its own accord. Whatever the case, we went on, the two of us, for some time, my solo less a solo than a duet, brass Lamb's dilated alarm somewhat sedated by Djamilaa's make-it-all-better remit.

The role I referred to as peculiar came in farther on. It was as I toyed with a string of inverted mordents that Djamilaa, having let her singing fade, raised her trumpet to her lips again. She fingered the valves and blew into the horn, matching what I played note for note, flurry for flurry — miming what I played, to be more exact, for though she fingered and blew not a sound came out. It was an odd, mimed or mute provocation or support which got even odder. Nothing at all came out at first but after a few bars a balloon emerged from the bell of the horn. The trumpet continued to emit no sound, albeit Djamilaa continued fingering and blowing, but a comic-strip balloon came out of the bell as if to show that, even though I thought I gave it little if any thought, bottle cap impact, if not impactedness, would not be denied its due. Inscribed in the balloon were these words: *Bottle cap suzerainty lifted its magic wand, a conductor's baton it tapped me on the shoulders with as if dubbing me a knight. A page, a prompter-in-waiting, arose with each tap, one on my left shoulder, one on my right.* This was greeted with scattered applause and exhortations from the audience, some of whom had no doubt heard about that night in Seattle, the now near-legendary night when Penguin blew such balloons.

Djamilaa and I took a breath at the same time and with that the balloon disappeared. Having taken a breath, we began to blow again at the same time. When we did another balloon emerged from the bell of Djamilaa's horn, a balloon in which one read: *Djbai and Bittabai they were called. Djbai stood on my left shoulder and whispered into my ear — spoke for rising pitch, asymptotic inflection. Bittabai stood on my right shoulder and whispered into my ear, speaking for stac-*

cato indentation. It was still only my horn that any sound came out of and it took next to no thinking about at all to realize, what with the advanced articulacy with which I now blew, that the words enclosed in Djamilaa's balloons were the words my trumpet spoke.

We were all, Djamilaa included, both pleased and taken aback, surprised and taken aback, by the return of the comic-strip balloons. Not a few heads were scratched, Djamilaa's and mine included, as to whether she put words in my mouth or I put words in hers. Whatever the case, we again took a breath at the same time, whereupon the second balloon disappeared. When we again, at the same time, began to blow another balloon emerged, this one, with its Penguin spin, raising further questions as to who had whose two cents' worth in whose mouth: *They vied like devil and angel locked in quantum coalescence, less devil and angel, on deeper inspection, than fire and light. I lay flat on the floor, brought back to life by the bottle cap's hum, but in what the hum said I saw myself run over, having walked all day at loose ends up and down Djeannine Street, the one serious risk I had ever taken or would ever take it seemed at the time.* I looked at Penguin, who smiled and seemed on the verge of laughing. When Djamilaa and I took a breath the balloon disappeared.

People in the audience were now on the edges of their seats, some of them holding their breath it appeared. Djamilaa and I blew again at the same time and out came a balloon bearing these words: *The car I saw myself run over by was the car Jarred Bottle sat in waiting for the traffic light to change — turn red, yellow and green at the same time. Djbai stood on his left shoulder shouting go, Bittabai on his right shouting stop. He was waiting for them to say the same thing at the same time, the car, unmoving, running over me nonetheless.* Again we took a breath at the same time and the balloon disappeared. Again when we resumed blowing a new balloon emerged: *I was what moved. Flat on my back, I slid along under the car, a quasi-conveyor-belt I could've sworn I saw Djeannine running in place on. I now no longer walked the street, I was the street. Bottle cap adamance hummed underneath me, stroked my back, my spine a string struck dulcimerlike by bottle cap suzerainty's magic wand.*

The return of the comic-strip balloons provided more than ample food for thought. Bottle cap impactedness had gone underground it appeared, but only to emerge with all the more finesse, all the more bouyancy, only to rise like a balloon or as a balloon, subterranean strum calibrating the hum of which balloon number three spoke and to which balloon number five returned. As it rose it also evidently picked up or picked up on the gauntlet I had thrown down, dubbing me a knight before extending a chivalrous conveyor-belt street on which Djeannine walked and/or ran in place. Djamilaa's bottle cap launching bend had been some sort of grounding device which evidently made her the channel thru which chthonic strum's ventriloquial élan issued forth. I had less than a moment to chew and digest this and what other food the balloons' return provided for thought, for Penguin, I heard and saw, had taken his horn to his mouth and was now preening, punctuating and embroidering the Djeannine Street line I'd ventured upon. This was clearly turf he took to be his or at least turf he took it he knew a thing or two about. Clearly he wanted in—indeed, was already there, I heard his alto insist.

Penguin's tone was a tart, mordacious thing which bit into the latter part of the run I played and continued on when Djamilaa and I again took a breath at the same time. He staked a claim during the pause we took, but the balloons were evidently no respecter of persons, for when Djamilaa and I resumed blowing this time no balloon emerged. Yes, it

was true that the balloons' first appearance had been out of
the bell of Penguin's horn on that phenomenal night in
Seattle his tart claim now insisted we recall. And, yes, it was
at least arguable that Penguin's broken-tooth addendum to
the Djeannine dream seemed to single him out, seemed to
give him special status, even seemed, as he now contended, to
have been the "open sesame" which gave us access to
Djeannine Street. Still, the balloons were not to be sum-
moned by Penguin's increasingly proprietary boast, no matter
how heartfelt, no matter how heady, no matter that Djamilaa
and I went on in the very vein which had been so effective
before he jumped in. Proprietary claims had no place on post-
expectant ground, the balloons' non-emergence appeared to
insist — a caveat whose bearing upon tar pit premises didn't
escape one's notice. Tar was indeed the antithesis of post-
expectancy's non-attached address — anything but unstuck
one saw at once.

Though the wind had been somewhat taken out of our sails
we continued to play, press on, the music in a sense all the
more inspired in the face of the balloons' reticence and
refusal to emerge. Chastened a bit perhaps but clearly
undaunted, Penguin played with as much passion and preci-
sion as ever, soon indicating that Djamilaa and I should pull
back, let him take over. This we did and Penguin went from
embellishing voice to solo voice by adopting a somewhat drier
tone, picking his way thru a wry, reflective run whose admon-
itory tag turned proprietary boast on its head but was no less
heartfelt and no less heady for doing so. What was most
instructive was the way in which dryness gradually grew bit-
tersweet. Penguin, it seemed, wagged a bittersweet, admon-
ishing finger which bordered on tart, recalling Carlos Ward,
maybe early Robin Kenyatta somewhat, slurred sweetness
tolling the balloons' non-emergence, bidding them goodbye.

Penguin had now embarked on a Lamb/Lam dialectic of his own, bittersweet bleat implicitly vying with proprietary boast, the tart proprietary claims he'd embroidered the latter part of my solo with, the balloonless part. That the balloons had not come out for him he now parlayed into lamblike penance, a sheepish mien which over the long haul, however, built on a dry run of wit as well as on bittersweet bleat. He increasingly accented the fact that in this case the wind taken out of our sails was actually air let out of our balloons. This he did by literalizing lamblike penance (metaphorical boat no match for literal balloon) and by taking dry run literally as well.

It was as if tart giving way to bittersweet wasn't renunciative enough. It reached the point where he took the horn from his mouth, removed the mouthpiece, returned the horn to his mouth and blew, playing the rest of his solo that way, mouthpiece in his pocket. Unlike Djamilaa's balloon-accompanied blowing, which had been silent and to which the mouthpiece removal alluded, Penguin's alto, absent mouthpiece notwithstanding, emitted sound. One heard the air passing thru the horn, as if (the insinuation escaped no one) it was air being let out of a balloon.

Penguin blew and blew and blew—so much so, so taxingly so, one feared he would hyperventilate, pass out. Lost air, let-out air, was his text and he took no prisoners, preaching a long, no-letup sermon while Drennette and Aunt Nancy provided sober, unstinting support. Sackcloth and ashes couldn't have made his point any more graphically, but the audience couldn't quite agree on how to take his penitential tack, invested as it so deftly was with droll insinuation, witty vagary, dry jest. Some sat with long faces, lugubrious, withdrawn. Others wore an all-purpose grin, enjoying the spectacle no less than the wry humor woven into it. Others outright giggled, as though the air being let out of the balloon were laughing gas.

It was wild, for all its lamblike penitence, raucous — as wicked as it was witty. The giggles, in fact, gradually gained the upper hand, spreading throughout the audience, infectious even to the point of seizing those who sat with long faces. It reached the point where everyone in the audience sat giggling. Even Penguin, once it got to this point, looked out over the audience and grinned, notwithstanding the horn was still in his mouth. He seemed pleased, as though his intent had been to arrive at a giggly consensus, but soon it was more than this, soon he did more than grin. It reached the point where he too couldn't help giggling, though he continued blowing even so. His embouchure was now unsteady but he somehow managed to keep hold of the horn and to keep blowing, his blowing broken into by giggles, the infectious tickle which had taken hold.

The giggly vibration which now ran thru the room was hard to resist. It was all the rest of us in the band could do to keep from being swept up in it, but somehow each of us was able to keep a straight face. Drennette and Aunt Nancy went on providing austere, unstinting support, while Djamilaa, Lambert and I looked on without a hint of a giggle or a grin. The contrastive play between Penguin's giggly depletion and the calm, no-nonsense chorus we comprised made the audience giggle all the more, which in turn made it even more difficult for us not to giggle or grin.

Even so, we maintained our calm, no-nonsense aplomb. On the cue from Lambert we restated the head, albeit Penguin went on blowing sans mouthpiece, giggling, and then we brought the piece to an end with the paradelike passage. Notwithstanding so emphatic an ending (not unlike an exclamation point), Penguin went on blowing a bit longer, letting the sound of the air passing thru the horn gradually fade, giving himself the last word, no longer giggling.

Then there was silence for a moment or two. The applause, when it came, was loud and long. I found I couldn't help joining in — applauding, unbeknown to all but myself, my head's newly arrived at unimpactedness having withstood the giddy gauntlet Penguin threw down.

Yours,
N.

Dear Angel of Dust,

The balloons are words taken out of our mouths, an eruptive critique of predication's rickety spin rewound as endowment. They subsist, if not on excision, on exhaust, abstract-extrapolative strenuousness, tenuity, technical-ecstatic duress. They advance the exponential potency of dubbed excision—plexed, parallactic articulacy, vexed elevation, vatic vacuity, giddy stilt. They speak of overblown hope, loss's learned aspiration, the eventuality of seen-said formula, filled-in equation, vocative imprint, prophylactic bluff. They raise hopes while striking an otherwise cautionary note, warnings having to do with empty authority, habitable indent, housed as well as unhoused vacuity, fecund recess.

The balloons are love's exponential debris, "high would's" atmospheric dispatch. Hyperbolic aubade (love's post-expectant farewell), they arise from the depth we invest in ordeal, chivalric trauma — depth charge and buoy rolled into one. They advance an exchange adumbrating the advent of optic utterance, seen-said exogamous mix of which the coupling of tryst and trial would bear the inaugural brunt. Like Djeannine's logarithmic flute, they obey, in the most graphic imaginable fashion, ocular deficit's oracular ricochet, seen-said remit.

The balloons are thrown-away baggage, oddly sonic survival, sound and sight rolled into one. They map even as they mourn post-appropriative precincts, chthonic or subaquatic residua come to the surface caroling world collapse. They dredge vestiges of premature post-expectancy (overblown arrival, overblown goodbye), seen-said belief's wooed risk of inflation, synaesthetic excess, erotic-elegiac behest. The balloons augur

— or, put more modestly, acknowledge — the ascendancy of videotic premises (autoerotic tube, autoerotic test pattern), automatic stigmata bruited as though of the air itself.

Such, at least, was the insistence I heard coming out of Dolphy's horn. "The Madrig Speaks, the Panther Walks" was the cut. I sat down to listen to it only minutes ago and found myself writing what you've just read. Never had Eric's alto sounded so precocious and multiply-tongued, never so filled with foreboding yet buoyant all the same, walk (panther) and talk (madrig) never so disarmingly entwined.

Listening, more deeply than ever, bone-deep, I knew the balloons were evanescent essence, fleet seen-said equiva-lence, flighty identity, sigil, sigh. This was the horn's bone-deep indenture, wedge and decipherment rolled into one. This could only, I knew, be the very thing whose name I'd long known albeit not yet found its fit, the very thing which, long before I knew it as I now know it, I knew by name—the name of a new piece I'd write if I could.

What I wouldn't give, that is, to compose a piece I could rightly call "Dolphic Oracle." It would indeed ally song (madrig) with speech, as well as with catlike muscularity and sinew — but also with catlike, post-expectant tread, oxy-moronically catlike, post-expectant prowl, post-expectant pounce, an aroused, heretofore unheard of, hopefully seen-said panther-python mix. . .

Yours,

N.

Dear Angel of Dust,

Could be. Yes, possibly so. The balloons, for all their out-ward display and apparent address of popular wish (literal access, legible truth) may well, as you say, signal an inward turn. As I've said before, the last thing we want is to be a lonely hearts band, but that may in fact be what, under Penguin and Drennette's influence, we're becoming or may even have already become. Are the balloons' apparent roots in problematic romance, their repeated erotic-elegiac lament, a default on collectivist possibility, a forfeiture of possible bondings greater than two, an obsessed, compensatory return (would-be return) to pre-post-romantic ground?

I don't know. I'm not so sure, for one thing, it can all be laid at Penguin and Drennette's feet. To whatever extent the balloons embody a retreat from more properly collectivist wishes, an introspective move masquerading as wished-for romance, costume-courtly complaint, the larger social, politi-cal moment we find ourselves in would have to have had a hand in it, no? I don't much subscribe to the increasing talk, in these dreary times, of "empowerment," "subversion," "resistance" and so forth. I once quoted Bachelard's line, "Thirst proves the existence of water," to a friend, who answered, "No, *water* proves the existence of water." I find myself more and more thinking that way. I find myself—and this goes for everyone else in the band, I think—increasingly unable (albeit not totally unable) to invest in notions of dialec-tical inevitability, to read the absence of what's manifestly not there as the sign of its eventual presence. To whatever extent hyperbolic aubade appears to have eclipsed collective "could," the balloons' going on about love's inflated goodbye should alert us to the Reaganomic roots of that eclipse.

I drove down to Santa Ana yesterday. An old friend and I went to the store at one point and on our way we passed a neighborhood park which has more and more become a camp for the homeless. Park Avenue people now call it, irony their one defense. Anyway, as we drove past, my friend, looking out the window, sneered, "Look at them, a bunch of dialects." He meant "derelicts." So much for malaprop speech as oppositional speech, I couldn't help thinking, so much for oppositional *any*thing.

That's how I sometimes feel, how we all sometimes feel. Not all the time, but often enough to nourish what you call an inward turn. I don't altogether buy your inward/outward split, but if you're saying the balloons' erotic-elegiac lament mourns the loss of larger bonding as well, I agree.

Yours,

N.

PS: What the two occasions the balloons have emerged on have in common is the ur-foundational/anti-foundational sense and/or apprehension we had—atomistic ledge/needling mist/pointillist plank-walk in Seattle, subterranean strum/ "collapsed" contour/tar pit premises at Keystone Korner. Each entailed an excavation of substrate particles or precincts, erstwhile plummet or plunge. Are the balloons mud we resurface with, mud we situate ourselves upon, heuristic precipitate, axiomatic muck, unprepossessing mire? I ask because of my acquaintance with earth-diver myths—myths in which an animal plunges into primeval waters and brings up a mouthful or a beakful of mud, mud from which the world is then made. In some the animal is a tortoise, in others a boar, in others a duck, in others a loon. Could the balloons, I'm asking, be a pseudo-

Bahamian play on the latter, namesake play with B'-*Ba* over-
tones, the spirit or the embodied soul of namesake play going
by the name B'Loon?

I say yes. B'Loon, not unrelated to Djbouche, is our murky,
mired cry, a call for world reparation. It muddies our mouths
with the way the world is even if only to insist it be otherwise.
Such insistence notwithstanding, it implicates us (myth
advancing mud, mouth proving mud) in the pit we'd have it
extricate us from.

Dear Angel of Dust,

Djamilaa says Turner was wrong. We worked on "Tosaut
L'Ouverture" at rehearsal last night and I got to talking about
how the piece came about. Lately we haven't been getting the
sense of subtle, unsounded shout I had in mind when I wrote
it. We managed it early on, but the last few times we've played
the piece on gigs I've noticed a certain overstatement creep-
ing in, as though the band had read but misread my mind
regarding shout, taken it literally, a matter of volume rather
than bend (circumambular bend, oblique, steal-away torque).
I pointed this out last night after we ran thru the piece once
and the overstatement, as on recent gigs, was there again.
Hoping it would help, I related in detail what had brought
"Tosaut L'Ouverture" about, which I hadn't before to anyone
but you. When I got to Turner's idea that the use of the word
"shout" to refer to circumambular movement derives from
the Arabic word *saut*, Djamilaa said no, that couldn't be, that
saut isn't pronounced like "shout" and that it doesn't mean to
walk around the Ka'aba, it means voice, sound.

I thought about it a while and then said it was no problem,
that *saut* not being pronounced like "shout" actually made the
point I was trying to make, albeit differently, that *saut*, not
sounding like "shout," implies the turn toward unsounded
shout I wanted us to bring to "Tosaut L'Ouverture." "Let it be
our boat," I found myself saying, "a bend at the heart of sound
we ride like an ark, weather like a storm, a calm, contrary eye
to see us thru." I said that meaning bent toward movement
rather than sound was what whatever shout the piece calls for
wants — an arced, inostensible shout, inostensible decree.
Inostensible decree, I went on, was a proviso issued at the

heart of sound which allowed fertile mistakes like Turner's
saut/shout derivation, the phonic license which made it possi-
ble to imagine *saut* might have been (mis)pronounced "shout."
"Especially," Aunt Nancy chimed in, "given the phonic liber-
ties transported Africans have been known to take."

"Rather than take shout literally," I eventually concluded,
"treat it like a mistake that's bound to be made and that one
both wants and doesn't want to make. Remember that the
'shout'—the *saut*—in 'Tosaut' has to do with a detour thru rel-
ativizing salt. Remember that salt gives its grain of truth a
renunciative spin. Remember that shout posed as movement
rather than sound is a way of dancing by another name." It was
one of my more inspired exhortations, a quick mix of admoni-
tion and provocation I wouldn't have thought I could come up
with had I not heard myself do so. And it did make a differ-
ence. "Tosaut L'Ouverture," when we now ran thru it, was a
long devotional song tinctured with inklings of angular remit.
Post-expectant distraint, a rare breed of longing, qualified our
sound by way of an arced, immaterial itch with which it
invested each note. Tosaut horses did indeed run, as though
itch were the constituent meat they were made of, not unlike
the carousel of notes I saw circling my head after drinking *saut*
soup. We were definitely a whole lot closer to my conception
of the piece — all the more so the third time we ran thru it,
which we got on tape, a copy of which I've enclosed.

I write as well to say that word has been spreading about the
balloons. The Seattle gig created a bit of a stir but it seems to
have taken the Keystone Korner appearance to convince peo-
ple the balloons are no fluke. Their second appearance appears
to have made the point that they're for real, a force to contend
with, and the scene has been more and more abuzz with talk of
them over the past three weeks. As you yourself have done,
many people have asked questions about them, ranging from

technical (how do we do it) to philosophic (what do they mean), some posing them directly to us, others bandying questions as well as theories about on a grapevine which ultimately makes its way to us. We could see something like this coming back when the balloons first appeared on the Seattle gig and we decided the best thing would be to maintain a public silence, not respond to the talk, something we now see we're not able to do.

We've gotten requests for interviews from some of the music journals and have started to get phone calls from newspeople at a few TV and radio stations. We've turned them all down. We've also, however, come under attack by some who say the balloons are a gimmick, a ploy, an attempt to go commercial, that we're turning ourselves into a circus act. It's in the face of this development we find we can't keep quiet. That the balloons are being taken the wrong way, by the well-meaning as well as the not-so-well-meaning, became clear a couple of days ago when we got a call from NuMu in New York, the place we played last November. They wanted us to come back for a two-week stint, but the owner, after talking a while about dates, pay and such, said, "By the way, be sure to bring the balloons"—which would've been funny had he not been serious. He wanted to write it into our contract that the balloons had to appear at least once a night.

How much our silence has had to do with things getting so out of hand we can't say, but their having done so requires we speak up. To that end, we decided to issue a press release. It was agreed I should be the one to write it, which I did, with editorial input from the rest of the band. We've sent it out to all the newspapers, wire services, radio and TV stations, music journals and so forth. I enclose a copy for you.

As ever,

N.

POST-EXPECTANT PRESS RELEASE #1

In view of discussions now going on concerning the balloon sightings at two of our recent performances, we, the Molimo m'Atet, feel impelled to break our silence regarding the matter. We now issue the first in a possible series of press releases. We will issue others if the need arises, as the need arises. There has been a great deal of talk and speculation generated by the two performances and we speak now to respond to questions which have been posed to us and to dispel certain misunderstandings which are going around as to the nature and import of the balloons' emergence. These inquiries dwell on questions of origin and motive, so let us state at the outset that the balloons are not, as some have alleged, a gimmick, a publicity stunt, a cheap trick we hope to cash in on. The charge of sellout is the last we should have to answer, but that there are those who will stop at nothing to explain mystery away comes as no surprise. By this we mean to suggest, to those genuinely interested in where the balloons come from, that their roots, as far as we can tell, are coincident with the world, that they afford no abstraction or extrapolation away from the post-expectant, post-explanatory fact of their being here.

Mystery notwithstanding, post-explanatory fact, in this instance, bears a name—a name which reminds us of certain risks we run with naming, a name which risks inflation as well as tautology: B'Loon. B'Loon is the bird that dives under the water at the beginning of things, fills its beak with mud at the bottom and then comes back up. It's from B'Loon's beakful of mud that the world is made. Rather than explain, B'Loon expands upon murky origins. According to some, for example,

B'Loon was once a man, a fisherman in fact. He and another fisherman quarreled one day while out at sea in their canoes. B'Loon had caught several fish and the other fisherman, having caught none, knocked him on the head, cut out his tongue and took his catch. When B'Loon reached shore he could only cry like a loon and the Great Spirit, hearing his cry, turned him into a loon. His quasi-human cry recalls his having once been a man, as well as the wrong he suffered at the other fisherman's hands.

Others, however, insist B'Loon was at first a loon and that he became a man at a certain Kuloscap's behest, having served faithfully as Kuloscap's servant, during which tenure Kuloscap taught him his distinctive quasi-human cry. Still others argue that B'Loon had been a boar before becoming a loon and a tortoise before becoming a boar, that B'Loon's roots go all the way back to Mesopotamia. Some say that B'Loon's footprints inspired cuneiform writing, though others dispute this, arguing that B'Loon didn't become a loon until long after leaving the Fertile Crescent. Even so, the belief persists among some that the world arose not from a founding beakful of mud but from founding footprints left in the mud, that the world began with writ, B'Loon's wedge-like tracks.

We, the Molimo m'Atet, see no reason to choose. B'Loon, true muse of inclusion, rolls earthen writ and airborne whoosh into one, earthen wedge and airborne oomph into one, subaquatic beak and airborne word into one. B'Loon marries flight with mired cry, height with depth, depth with height, heaven-piercing beak with aboriginal mud, fecund muck, footloose, itinerant word with graven earth. Thus it is that B'Loon is said to be intimate with air, the atmosphere's doings, weather, said to be able to forecast rain. This, we now know, cuts both ways. Thus it was that a low-lying mist fol-

lowed us into Soulstice that night in Seattle — a metathetic
prediction auguring B'Loon's imminent advent.

B'Loon's comings and goings, however, we can neither
predict nor control. As Byard Lancaster said in the title of one
of his albums: it's not up to us. B'Loon indicts presumptions
of command as it bestows command, as though command
were its own false twin, seeded cloud the false face of rain
save that ceded command antithetically intervene. By no
means an easy muse or master, B'Loon requires that grasp
and relinquishment meet, that they wrestle the angel each
takes the other to be, the devil each takes the other to be — a
harlequin fray in which debt mires endowment, advancing an
ethic of letting go while suggesting letting go might be an
ulterior tack aimed at taking hold, taking hold a Pyrrhic
seizure not unmixed with letting go, each the other's taint and
contagion, ad infinitum. B'Loon ushers the soul of blown
seizure, fractured access, reach and retreat.

Whether "man" first and "bird" later or vice versa, B'Loon
is both "man" and "bird," an avatar of broken bonds, the break
both advance and ordeal. B'Loon's quasi-human cry recalls the
attack he suffered but also aligns articulate squawk with legi-
ble scratch, inscribed earth with contentious air, wedge with
complaint. Whether as wing or as wedge, B'Loon augurs an
opportune prodigal opening conducive to broken bond as
qualitative breakthrough, quantum slip. Whether as wing or
as wedge, squawking slip bridges seen/said chasm — wishfully
most often but for real at B'Loon's behest. Squawking slip rolls
wing and wedge into one, scrawl and scratch into one, witness
and plaintiff into one, wind and writ into one.

Sibling wind and sibling witness (Sun Ra said it years ago:
"My Brother the Wind"), B'Loon yields mended kinship,
mended membership, mends otherwise broken bonds.
B'Loon blows thru every exhaustion, a second wind not

unequatable with fugitive spirit, fertile exhaust, bent on depletion being the ground for new growth. We get lucky every now and then and blow with it.

Dear Angel of Dust,

Turner was right. Djamilaa and I have gone into the shout/*saut* matter further and the problem turns out to be that the word rendered *Saut* in Parrish's book doesn't appear that way in his. Parrish uses an *S* instead of the phonetic symbol ʃ that Turner uses ("voiceless palato-alveolar fricative, like *sh* in English *shame*"). In the passage she refers to, Turner writes with regard to "shout": "Cf. Ar., ʃaut 'to move around the Kaaba (the small stone building at Mecca which is the chief object of the pilgrimage of Mohammedans) until exhausted'; ʃauwata 'to run until exhausted.'" There is in fact an Arabic *saut*, which, as Djamilaa pointed out, means voice, sound, but we now see that's not the word Turner meant. The dictionary we consulted says that ʃaut is a race to a goal, also the course or the track over which a race takes place. It's not hard to see how it could have come to refer, in idiomatic usage, to the course taken around the Ka'aba. That it was applied to the course taken by participants in the ring shout is also easy to understand, especially given the presence of Muslims in the Sea Islands. In the context of cross-cultural sanction and subterfuge brought about by the slave trade, it makes perfect sense. The phonic distinction between sound and movement in Arabic (*saut* and ʃaut) is maintained but all but lost in its intersection with "shout"—to say nothing of its application to a form of movement, the ring shout, which is decidedly not without sound. The distinction is, in effect, silent, as is the admission that the shout isn't only sound but also movement—that is, a dance.

Not that "Tosaut L'Ouverture" would be any less valid had Turner been wrong. Its tenability is one of generative divergence, the bend away from pat equivalence exemplified by nonsonant shout. It was incorrect but not a mistake, a mistake but a fertile mistake, to read the "-saut" in "Tosaut" as though it was Turner's ∫*aut*. "The accuracy of the bow is judged by its curve," Ibn 'Arabi says.

Yours,
N.

Dear Angel of Dust,

There's a new wrinkle on the balloon front. A photographer has come forth claiming to have been at Keystone Korner the night the balloons made their second appearance. He says he took photos of them or at least thought he had until he developed the film. He says he could find no trace of them on either the negatives or the prints. Everything else—the band, the instruments, the stage and so forth—came out fine, but the balloons were nowhere to be seen. He doesn't question that they were actually there that night — he saw them, no doubt about that, he insists—but this "new revelation," as some are now calling it, has added to the controversy surrounding the balloons. Doubters are calling the sightings a case of mass hysteria, arguing not that none of us saw what we say we saw but that what we saw was a collective hallucination. The camera doesn't lie they insist.

I wanted to issue another press release addressing this new information and the doubts to which it's given rise, but no one else in the band thought it a good idea. It's too soon after the first release, they told me, and, besides, we can't spend our time arguing with the doubters and the critics, responding every time something new comes up—a view I came around to without much fuss. Still, I'd like to have publicly made the point that the balloons' refusal to show up on the photographs (it's a refusal, not a failure, I'd insist) calibrates a distinction between mechanical gaze and organic sight. This "new revelation" has caused me to rethink my assertion that the balloons "acknowledge the ascendancy of videotic premises." I'm glad they turn out to be camera-shy, and I hope, if they ever show up again, they'll continue to be. That B'Loon is neither photogenic nor, one would assume, telegenic, that, rather than a failing, this augurs the rejection of telecom charisma, is a point which might've been worth pursuing in a "Post-Expectant Press Statement #2," an intermittent feature of which would have been a soft phonologic focus allowing *camera* and *chimera* to blend, bleed into each other, *chimeric* and *charismatic* to do so as well.

I would have started it something like this: "B'Loon stood at the podium holding a pointer—part magic wand, part conductor's baton, a pointer nonetheless. On the blackboard behind him, scrawled in chalk, was the inscription 'B'Lam!,' below which, also scrawled in chalk, was a dash followed by the words 'Namesake Exclamation #1.' B'Loon, charismatic mage, cleared his throat, turned to his left and pointed to the writing on the blackboard, still not having spoken yet." I would have gone on to identify B'Lam as anagrammatic Lamb apostrophized, called out to as kin. I'd have called it a loonlike cry, personified, protesting capture, demanding immediate release. I'd have called it the avatar of onomatopoetic impact (rough and ready command, camera-ready chimera), gone on to write something like this: "B'Loon, chimeric bird/man mix, invoked the avatar of onomatopoetic impact, hoping to go over big, hoping he'd be a hit, during this the taping of his appearance on 'The Tonight Show.' He'd been nervous for days, weeks, months. It thus came as no surprise that during the drive to Burbank there had been moths, not butterflies, in his stomach and that his stomach might as well have been wool. He stood now, nervous as ever, charismatic albeit camera-shy, all the more chimeric, about to embark upon the lecture he'd been invited to present, or so everyone thought."

I'd have then gone on to devote a good deal of space to B'Loon's inner state, the anxiety and the apprehension that plague him, the qualms, the insistent self-questioning he

faces regarding the propriety of such an appearance. I'd have
taken my time evoking the fraught vessel he feels himself to
be (rough and ready charisma, ready-or-not chimera), taken
pains to evoke the stage fright he suffers, gone to great
lengths to evoke the camera-shy refuge he seeks turning
toward the blackboard behind him. With an exactitude
approaching camera-shy quanta, chimeric truth, I'd have then
dwelt on his moth-eaten stomach, offering image after image
aimed at suggesting the vertiginous pit he now feels it to be.
I'd have ended this stretch with something like this: "B'Loon
teetered on the brink of a precipice, the macrocosmic pit
implied by the moth-eaten pit his stomach now was. He
would have to dive down, go deep into that pit were he ever
to get his feet on new ground, gain a new footing. He would
brave the moth-eaten remains both outside and inside him-
self, raise the muck to higher ground, make of the muck some
higher ground."

I'd have gone on to point out that although at its deepest
reach macrocosmic pit meets cosmic shiver, the more imme-
diate cause of B'Loon's nervousness needs to be taken into
account. I'd have noted that B'Loon, quite private by nature,
intends to go public in an even bigger way than appearing on
"The Tonight Show" implies, much bigger, in fact, than he'd
ever dreamt he would until only a few days before. "B'Loon,"
I'd have written, "had more in mind than the lecture he'd
been invited to present. He had decided only a few days
before to put his 'Notes on Capillary Pneumatics' aside, to
cash in on his otherwise camera-shy charisma (chimeric
readiness) by using his appearance on such a widely viewed
program to announce his candidacy for president. He derived
a certain pedigree from Lester Young, of course, but the
write-in campaign, many years back, for a trumpeter with
whom he'd long felt a namesake rapport also bolstered his

resolve. The first words out of his mouth, he had decided, would be these: 'I largely owe the decision I'm about to announce to the ballooning cheeks of another bird/man mix's "worthy constituent." It's mainly, that is, because of Dizzy that I'm here to do what I'm about to do.' Only now, having cleared his throat again but still not having spoken, did he see that the debt he owed Dizzy ran deeper than even he knew. Vertiginous pit bespoke such depth, bore capacious witness to the namesake spin B'Loon increasingly felt himself caught up in, the giddy brink the moth-eaten ground on which he stood had brought him to, a giddiness which made him grab the podium for support."

I'd have needed to convey how anxious B'Loon is to get it over with, to get the announcement out of the way and to sit chatting with Johnny. That he actually looks forward to that conversation is a point worth making, one that I'd have pursued at some length. It shows that B'Loon's apprehensions have largely to do with the portentousness of public scale, that the one-on-one conversation format, albeit viewed by millions, offers a semblance of the intimate proportions he feels more comfortable with. B'Loon is there, that is, both to avail himself of and to in some degree temper the advance of telespeak. He's not so sure anymore, however, that he can pull it off, that he can actually, as he likes to put it, feed the beast without it biting off his hand. He feels, that is, less and less camera-ready. Chimeric readiness more and more turns camera shy. "B'Loon's would-be camera-ready charisma," I'd have gone on to write, "let him down. He more and more felt that mass-mediated stump stood in the way of genuine change. He cleared his throat yet again but instead of speaking stepped away from the podium, laid his pointer down, turned his back to the audience and the cameras and took the two steps it took to reach the blackboard. When he didn't feel on the verge of falling he felt on the verge of floating away, yet even so he managed to pick up a stick of chalk and to carefully, albeit a bit shakily, write the word *REVOLUTION*, all in caps, on the board. He also, with his other hand, picked up an eraser, with which, once he'd gotten the word written, he erased the *R*. Having erased the *R*, he now, with his chalk-holding hand, rewrote it, whereupon he promptly, with the eraser-holding hand, erased it again, only to write it again with the chalk-holding hand. He quickly established and sustained a rhythm wherein he alternately erased and rewrote the *R*. He thought of *REVOLUTION* as a neon sign whose *R* flickered off and on. He stood with his back to the audience and the cameras, still not speaking, still not having spoken, though the chalkdust, every now and then, made him ever so gently cough, clear his throat."

That's the way I'd have left him — standing close to the blackboard, slightly hunched over, writing and erasing the *R* again and again. That now he owed less to Dizzy than to Miles might have gone without saying, but most likely I'd have pointed it out anyway. B'Loon, camera-shy chimera, decides that what he's doing is the way it ought to be done. He continues to stand there, his back to the audience and the cameras, gently coughing or clearing his throat every so often but silent otherwise. He has no interest now in presenting a lecture or in making a speech, no interest in chatting with Johnny afterwards. This becomes apparent to everyone present after a while and the cameras stop rolling. B'Loon, intent only upon the *R*, the chalk and the eraser, eventually has to be carried off the stage.

Forgive me. I didn't intend to go on so. It turns out to be something that wouldn't quite let go, our decision not to issue another press statement notwithstanding. Call it "Suppressed Press Release #1."

We've also made another decision, decided to put a record out. The arrangements have all been made, the date set. We go into the recording studio in a month and a half, on Trane's birthday, September 23rd.

As ever,

N.

Dear Angel of Dust,

Drennette's blasé facade finally broke. Djamilaa tells me the two of them went for a walk on the beach yesterday, that in the course of that walk it became clear that her apparent post-expectancy is anything but post-. It became apparent, she says, that Drennette's post-expectant pose is just that, a pose. It was Santa Monica Beach they went for the walk on. Drennette had phoned her in the morning saying she felt "at loose ends," had asked if they could get together sometime that afternoon. She looked, when she came by to pick her up, like nothing out of the ordinary had happened, Djamilaa says. She looked no different, showed no signs of distress or disarray, nor did it ever become apparent that anything on the order of an occurrence had caused what she called her being "at loose ends" — anything of recent advent, that is, for it eventually became evident, Djamilaa says, that a longstanding malaise lay beneath her blasé facade, the same longstanding malaise she touched on a bit at the Merchant of Venice a few months back.

They were walking along the beach, close to the water, Djamilaa says. They came to a mound of kelp which had been left there by the tide and Drennette stopped, looking down at it, momentarily lost in thought, contemplating the tangle of branches and stems. After a moment's reflection she all but inaudibly sighed before saying (more to herself than to her, Djamilaa says), "Our legs used to entwine like that. Rick and I used to lie in bed with our legs entwined." She let it go at that as they resumed walking, going back to whatever it was they'd been talking about before she stopped. She let it go only for the time being it turned out. Every so often, Djamilaa says, she went back to it, filling any lull in the conversation by reminiscing out loud, "Rick and I would sleep with our legs tightly entwined. . . ." Tight entwinement, Djamilaa says, came into poignant, retrospective play with "loose ends," limbed entanglement so elegiacally evoked it retroactively lent "loose" a previously absent grist. Limbed reminiscence achieved a rough poetry at points, bordering on "Empty Bed Blues." "Our legs," Drennette announced, "crossed and recrossed each other, less kelp than kindling. We were one another's wood, one another's shed, sought shelter." She went back to this conceit time and again, Djamilaa says. "Rick was my wood," she'd say, "Rick was my shed, sought shelter" — incantatory, almost liturgical, albeit, unlike liturgy or incantation, discontinuous, interrupted, cut up. They'd be walking along, talking about music or clothes or how good it felt to get out to the beach, whatever, and the talk would tail off and they'd walk on in silence for a while. Drennette, after a while, would say, "Rick was my wood, my shed, the wood I schooled my axe on, not knowing I schooled my axe." Or she'd say, "We were each other's fire. Our legs warmed each other like flames, wood to one another's fire." Or she'd say, "Rick's promise of warmth seemed endless," limbed reminiscence's rough poetry bordering on "Someday My Prince Will Come." "Even now," she'd continue, "it's hard not to believe we'll eventually be together again."

Djamilaa says that the oddest thing was that when she'd respond to this, try to pursue Drennette's talk of Rick further, asking a question, voicing her concern, Drennette would change the subject, go back to talking about music or the new skirt she recently bought or how beautifully the gulls flew, whatever. She seemed bent on talking about Rick but resisted talking about Rick. Heartfelt loss vied with affected non-feeling. "What's done's done," was the closest she'd come to engaging Djamilaa's questions or concern. "No point in going

on about that." Surface acceptance, Djamilaa says, attempted
to fend off depth — deepseated longing, deepseated lament,
deep feelings of loss only partly put behind. The mounds of
kelp strewn along the beach were depth's reminders,
mnemonic triggers translating "loose ends" into revenant
limbs, ventral embrace. Limbed reminiscence gained its grain
of salt by posing kelp as kindling, its true grain or its gritty
truth mixing would-be return with suppositious wood. Rick
was wood and seaweed both — revenant body, salt entangle-
ment, ephemeral touch, unravelable embrace. Weed
(unwanted growth) complicated wood (revenant flesh-and-
blood), an aliquant reminder gotten deep under her skin
going even deeper as time went by.

Rick, her fixation on kelp insinuated, was Drennette's
Tosaut wood, erstwhile rock. His remembered legs had a hold
on her still, entangled her with Tosaut obduracy, Tosaut salt.
Not unlike Ouiot's withered limbs, her own legs grew weaker,
Tosaut wood become Tosaut toxin, saline immensity's con-
strictive "twin." Drennette's legs, Djamilaa says, betrayed her.
As they walked on, close to the water, wet sand feeling good
on their bare feet, Drennette actually fell not long after say-
ing, "No point in going on about that." Her legs buckled, gave
out under her, sending her to the sand, knees first. She broke
her fall with her knees and her hands, bounding back up at
once, as though quickly recovering could erase the fact of her
having fallen, upset with herself for having done so but pre-
tending it was no big thing. Djamilaa had let out a cry of some
sort as she fell, had made a move to catch hold of her and
keep her from falling or, failing that, help her back up off the
sand. Drennette shrugged off her offer of help, Djamilaa says,
attempting to mask her disarray by resuming her blasé facade.
Her rough poetry betrayed her however. "I must have tripped
over a strand of kelp," she announced, though a quick perusal

of the area where she'd fallen proved otherwise. It was an area bare of kelp. There was nothing there but sand.

Drennette's having tripped over a phantom strand of kelp (if that's what it was) only made the fact that "what's done" wasn't really done more abundantly clear. Her going on to put a positive, compensatory spin on her breakup with Rick, Djamilaa says, was impossible not to see thru. "A drummer uses all four limbs," she said not long after falling. "Rick and me breaking up gave me back my legs. He was the wood I schooled my axe on in more ways than I knew. Disentangling axe from wood was something I needed to do." Tight entwinement, she was now saying, had arrested her growth. It was a bud whose bloom was breakup. Breakup loosened her limbs. It was this which had made her the drummer she now is.

This, as you know, is a claim she's made before. At the Merchant of Venice she implied a link between concussive spill and percussive spirit, suggesting she really didn't get going as a drummer until after that final bike ride with Rick. Here though, Djamilaa says, the hollowness of it couldn't have rung louder. There was a straining, vacuous quality to it, she says, as frayed-edged as nervous laughter. It was clear she sought consolation in the idea that her drumming thrives on solitude. Following as it did upon her fall gave it an almost desperate air.

Our recent attention to "Tosaut L'Ouverture" had a hand in all of this, as I've already suggested (Tosaut wood, erstwhile rock, Tosaut toxin. . .). This became evident tonight when Drennette showed up at rehearsal with a composition she's written, the first time she's done so since joining the band. The name of it is "Tosaut Strut." It shows her bent on bearing out the claim she made at the beach. More lope than strut, it brings Dewey Redman's "Lop-O-Lop" to mind, a deliberate erasure on Drennette's part, one suspects, of the line between lope and lop.

Like Dewey's piece, "Tosaut Strut" brings drums-and-bass interplay to the forefront, an uptempo outing in which spasmic rolls puncture tonic declension, lopped rolls giving way to the bass's low note braiding adventitious furtherance with suppositious fall. Drennette's recourse to the cowbell all but gloats over adventitious furtherance's braided survival, excavating a ruminative in-and-under ebb in which the raveling lines' taut storage unloads. How she and Aunt Nancy manage to create so prodigal a sense of outmaneuvered collapse I don't know. How they pull off the digestive translation of lop into lope they pull off I don't know. Bent-legged lope, which I'm tempted to call it, doesn't do it justice. Nor does (even more tempting) lope-a-dope.

I'd send a tape but we haven't ironed all the wrinkles out yet. The horn parts are particularly tricky, difficult to get down — long, overarching lines pestered by intercalary divagations. Brazilian samba lays reminiscent vocality atop a no-regrets percussive "pillow" in a way Drennette seems to want "Tosaut Strut" to have learned from. She seems to have had a "stratic" attenuation in mind, superstructural stretch undermined and maintained by bittersweet voicings. It's as if she'll admit or acknowledge nostalgia only in the mouths of others. The horns' bittersweet voicings grant a grudging nod to limbed reminiscence, a discreet division of emotional labor whereby she both doffs and dons her blasé facade. But, as I've said, all the wrinkles have yet to be ironed out. For one, Penguin does alright during the unison horn passages but he draws a blank when his turn to solo comes.

I'll send a tape when we've worked it out.

Yours,
N.

Dear Angel of Dust,

Penguin continues to draw a blank when it comes to solo-
ing on "Tosaut Strut." Something inside him balks at the
revivalist tack written into the piece — the way the mournful
chorus the unison passages effect gives way to solos which
advance a sense of renascent vigor, born-again legs gaining
higher ground. It's not hard to imagine what that something
is. The persistence of Drennette's memories of Rick no doubt
bothers him, though there's an aspect of it he's encouraged by
as well. Such persistence shows her, blasé facade notwith-
standing, to be not quite the post-expectant number she pre-
tends to be. He's more than ready to play his part in the
mournful chorus, to lament and lay such memories to rest.
But the laying-to-rest "Tosaut Strut" intends to advance
means to rise above rather than move on. It wants to anaes-
thetize present feeling rather than make way for it by leaving
past feeling behind. It wants to leave all feeling behind, all but
a feeling for the drums. It's to that that Penguin balks at lend-
ing himself. Thus the blank he draws when it's his turn to solo.

He hasn't come right out and said any of this. "For some
reason, I simply draw a blank when it's my turn to solo," he
says, declining to elaborate or to venture a guess what that
reason might be. He says it in a flat, disinterested tone of
voice, his face as devoid of expression as his manner of speak-
ing. Does he don a blasé facade of his own or is it true he has
no idea why he draws a blank? Whichever, we've decided not
to force the issue. We've decided not to have him solo on
"Tosaut Strut." Since doing so we've made some headway on
the other wrinkles which need ironing out. I'll be able to send
you a tape of it soon.

And, yes, there continues to be a to-do surrounding the balloons. We're beginning to regret them having come into the music. Maybe undermine is more what they do than underwrite it we've begun to fear. At the very least, in the public eye they've upstaged it of late. A failed embrace of captionless being or a failure to abide by captionless being is a fact of contemporary life they perhaps alert us to by appealing to—nothing, that is, to cheer about.

As ever,
N.

WIND-ASSISTED DRUM-LAB READOUT
(DREAM SOLILOQUY)

In my head I composed a letter I knew by heart. It began in a way I knew by heart but didn't know I knew. I bit my lip not to mouth what I wrote out loud. So it was I resisted adventitious locution, the wafted remit I ran the risk of exacting were it the "open sesame" I wished it would be. "Dear Lag-Leg Vibe," I wrote, biting my lip.

I bit my lip, pressing pen to paper within the cardiognostic chamber my head had become. I erased it, only to write it again, "Dear Lag-Leg Vibe." Biting my lip made the marks on the paper stay put.

Voices told me mud was my middle name but I bore it well. Namesake slippage muddied my mouth as I stood my ground, bitten lip bitten all the more intently, all but bleeding, mud a kind of blood, blood mud's afterthought. I bit my lip so intently it eventually began to bleed. It was then that I finally let up, loosened up.

When I loosened my embouchure, no longer bit my lip, a balloon rose from the page on which I wrote. As it rose it took the words up off the page I wrote them on. *Dear Lag-Leg Vibe*, written in the balloon, floated above the page, as did the rest of what I wrote: *That the balloons embody a wished-for return to primal mud there can be no doubt, but that such return makes mud sublime needs to be remembered. The balloons revisit mud only to take it higher, ostensible ascent so inextricably coincident with going down mud would appear to make sight "say's" recompense. Mud would so appear to clarify "say" we see words in the air.*

It was a reminder I wrote myself, something one might

tape to a refrigerator door. I wrote it while serving customers
in the kissing booth, the booth I stood in selling kisses and
Kashmiri Cough Drops. Middle name notwithstanding, my
name was Djeannine. Mud, my middle name, was the name
of the funky lipstick I wore. Mud brought all the way from the
Nile, the ads insisted—dark, alluvial lipstick laid on thick like
a sloppy kiss.

A dreamer licked my sister's pubic lips a million light-years
away and with every kiss I flexed my mouth with that dreamer's
abandon, loosening and stretching my lips, jaws and tongue,
doing all I could to give my clients their money's worth. My lips
covered their lips but would neither stick, stay nor settle, would
instead wander past corner-of-the-mouth, stray beyond lip-
ridge, kiss less what it was than lip-smear, mouth-smother,
leave a snail's trail of spit. Dark, alluvial lipstick muddied their
faces. No customer left my booth unsatisfied.

But, no, I was not Djeannine, I only dreamt I was. Dreamt
name notwithstanding, my name was Drennette. My tongue
was as wet as an old rope. My lips, dry as wood, resisted
kisses. My ass was as hard as a man's.

I wrote what I wrote not between customers in the kissing
booth but between beats. Stand wasn't what I did; I sat.

A snake's head buried beneath the stool on which I sat
would've sunk its fangs into my hips had my ass not been so
hard. Long hours at the drumset made it so. Many a hand
sought passage up my leg, under my dress, but only the drum-
mer's stool felt my rump, the insides of my thighs, only it got
anywhere near my private parts. Many a man tried to look up
my dress while I played but the drumset blocked their view.

Mud, on the other hand, occluded speech but in so doing
made it more clear, no longer transparent. Mud was loose
interstitial cement, my dream's loose translation of the space
between beats. It was the hair sticking out from the rein-

forced crotch of Djeannine's white panties, thetic aria ("air") to their whiteness's antithetic "earth."

Mud, I sang, was all name, only a name. Mud was middleness, founding glue. Name tied my tongue and tore my tongue, taut cord binding an otherwise unbound "earth," agitational cartwheel, blinding white spin.

My name was Drennette. I dreamt of Djeannine, dreamt I was Djeannine. My loose lips delivered spendthrift kisses, prodigal kisses. My tongue was a leaf of kelp, salty-sweet.

I sang an earthy aria, a foul-mouthed aria, fulfilling every customer's wish to be talked dirty to.

My salty tongue made lewd suggestion after lewd suggestion. My saucy mouth talked as nasty a talk as could ever be talked, notwithstanding my name was Drennette (Drennette Virgin to some, DV, Diva).

My high notes harbored B'Loon's beakful of mud.

Dear Angel of Dust,

Working out all the wrinkles introduced a new wrinkle. Scroll and teleprompted script rolled into one, B'Loon's most recent visit took an unexpected turn. What I wrote above is what it seemed I saw written in the blank Penguin had previously drawn on "Tosaut Strut." It was a blank he no longer drew but which it seemed I saw when I closed my eyes shortly into his solo. Yes, he finally soloed on "Tosaut Strut." How this came to be I could hardly wait to write you about. I could wait to write you the script I saw even less.

It happened at a place in town we played earlier tonight (last night really — it's two in the morning now), a place known as The Studio, over in the Crenshaw. Having finally worked out all the wrinkles, we were anxious to play "Tosaut Strut" before a live audience. Things were going well (nice turnout, serious listeners, everyone's chops up), so we gave it a go late in the second set.

We had ended the first set with "Tosaut L'Ouverture." The "lag along" regard for what gets away I've spoken of before in regard to the piece was very much in evidence in the reading we gave it. I hadn't realized before how much the music of my childhood had made an impact on the composition, but Drennette did something she hadn't done before, a subtle something which made me do just that. Every now and then, that is, she would drag the tip of one of her sticks across the snare drum's head, an explicit "lag along" tack she managed to work in without missing a beat. She worked in more than that, however, more than she knew (though, who can say, maybe not), for the very first time she did it I thought of a dance which was popular when I was ten known as "The Stroll." It was a dance in which dancers formed two parallel lines, down the "aisle" between which, a couple at a time, they promenaded. Part stroll, part extended stagger, the promenade featured a gangly, sideways carriage and a crossover step in which one foot was dragged on its side. "Tosaut L'Ouverture's" resistant lag, I realized, owes as much to this as to anything else. I thought of Chuck Willis's "Betty and Dupree," the way the mournful, coaxing sax appears to lament a lost instinctual rapport of some sort. I knew that lament had no doubt informed my piece's "lag along" chagrin.

The noncalibrated apportionment or appeal of "Tosaut L'Ouverture," the "lag along" vibe it adumbrated or advanced, hung in the air throughout the intermission and hung there as well throughout the second set. It hung with pointed incompletion and weight, albeit ever so lightly, especially so when we lit into "Tosaut Strut." It was as if we'd planned ahead — which, in a sense, we had, though with an

odd, unwitting prescience that went well beyond obvious
namesake tether. We had a feeling we were in for something
special the moment Drennette's drumsticks hit the skins. She
wasted no time weaving "lag along" vibe and lop-o-lop
resilience together as one, relating, with unheard-of articu-
lacy, blown matrimonial stroll and aborted bike ride, lag-leg
encumbrance and renascent strut. Betty to Rick's Dupree,
she wove an alternative tale, one of alternativity itself.

Drennette made it clear right away that the phantom
strand which had broken her stride at the beach was the pedal
which had broken during her final bike ride with Rick.
Revenant pedal floated up from the drums as though up from
under the sand, an inflated premise bent on regaining lost
ground, revenant beachhead, surge cut with imminent sashay.
The pedal proved a Pyrrhic encumbrance—aliquant landing
and "lag along" limb rolled into one, leapt-over strand (she
leapt, not fell, she insisted) whereby we became a septet. We
were seven, newly membered, paralegged. Doppelganger
strut so exacted leg from *leapt* we became a "steptet." Rick
ran with us it seemed.

In that sense, Rick running with us, we were back to being
six rather than seven. So palpable was his presence, so
impressive the music's evocation of theretofore lost but now
revenant legs, it made Penguin pretty much bow out, daunted
by what he took to be his rival's return (rival memory, revival-
ist "would"). Rick ran with us, thickly part of the pack, the
"steptet," and to the extent that he did Penguin withdrew,
blowing so faintly during the unison passage he could hardly
be heard. Coming out of that passage, Lambert lit into his
solo, a blistering foray in which he took no prisoners.
Following that came the next unison passage, a long,
labyrinthine excursion in which Penguin blew even more
faintly than before. He played as though he wasn't there, as

though Rick had taken his place. Him having withdrawn, we were again, "steptet" though we were, only six.

It was during this long, labyrinthine unison passage that Aunt Nancy made a decisive move, a move that brought about results beyond her wildest hopes. Penguin stood not far in front of her and a bit to her right, which made it easy for her, taking a step out from behind her bass while continuing to play, to lean forward and whisper into his ear. He had played his part in the unison passage lethargically up to this point, all but not blowing, all but announcing he wasn't there. After Aunt Nancy whispered into his ear, however, he perked up as if called back from nodding out. He now blew full force, his tone biting and robust. It even seemed his clothes fit him better, that he filled them out in exactly the way that, withdrawn, all but begging off being there, he hadn't since the advent of Rick's revenant legs.

Penguin's rehabilitation went even farther, however. As we neared the end of the long unison passage he made eye contact with me, whose turn it was to solo next, taking his right hand from the horn momentarily and pointing to himself, indicating by that that he wanted to solo. This took me by surprise but I gave him the nod to go ahead. When the unison passage ended he hit the upbeat like a diver hitting a springboard, then pulled back a microbeat almost at once, lopped ictus and lag-leg lope rolled into one. Drennette, gratified by his recourse to her lop/lope conceit, splashed a rubber-wrist flourish on cymbals by way of acknowledgement, then quickly got back to making her lag-leg rounds. A gimp-leg dip, that is, came around with the persistence of an oblong wheel, an asymmetric wheel Penguin rolled with at first and then, five bars later, climbed aboard and rode.

A rickety mix of ride and run, "Tosaut Strut" lived up to its name nonetheless. Aunt Nancy played "lag along" tag, a walking figure which caught Drennette's dip every other bar. Walking bass catching oblong wheel's apogee seemed to whoa ride's runaway drift somewhat. It brought containment to a pace which at times bordered on frantic, reining in run's unchecked furtherance of itself. More than that, it asserted a cocksure composure in full accord with eponymic strut.

Penguin plays bari on "Tosaut Strut," a horn he got around on, this time out, as though it were a tenor. It wasn't so much that he spent a good deal of time high up on the horn as that he made one think of Ornette's statement that the tenor is a rhythm instrument, made one think of the bari as a rhythm instrument too. He brought Fred Anderson to mind the way he motored so nimbly, nonchalantly even, in so frequently oblique a rapport with Drennette and Aunt Nancy's in-and-under ebb.

For all the time he spent up high on the horn Penguin more than gave the bottom its due. He had a cascading way of getting there and, once there, proffered a dark, thick sound which, viscosity notwithstanding, moved around with an inflection and fluidity more typical of the horn's middle range. Suggesting sludge without at all seeming sluggish, it was as thick as Turkish coffee, with all the kick of Turkish coffee, a dark, ever advancing bulb of sound.

Drennette ingeniously buffed Penguin's bulb of sound with intermittent strings of hissed rescission on high hat, clipped hisses which became a kind of chatter, an ongoing bug she put in Penguin's ear. Buffed bulb gave a glint or gleam to the otherwise dark, ever advancing brew, a philosophico-metallic sheen which led the way as it illumined our way.

Drennette's hissing chatter recalled the drummer we heard in Griffith Park somewhat—enough so, at any rate, to make me close my eyes. I was curious not so much to see whether I'd see the dancing broom as simply to see, as

Rahsaan once put it, what I could see. Her clipped hisses stirred up fairy dust, it seemed, a pharmacopoeic endowment (closed-eye, open-sesame inducement or endowment) one sensed was now in the air.

The first thing I saw when I closed my eyes was that the blank Penguin had previously drawn when it came to soloing on "Tosaut Strut" was indeed a drawn blank, that it lay within lines drawn horizontally and vertically which marked off a space which was rectangular in shape, less tall than it was wide. These lines merely formed a template, however, a frame for what, now that Penguin was soloing, unfolded or unrolled within the space they circumscribed.

That Penguin now played with new fluency and rare articulacy I already knew. How new and how rare I was about to find out. Drennette's clipped hisses both stirred up dust and splashed or spewed forth mud—dust in my eye, mud in Penguin's ear. She lent a taste of earth to his Turkish coffee, but, more than that, she sustained a burr, a buzz, a ring of resonant chatter, so insistently put the proverbial bug in his ear he rose to new heights—heights of uncanny intelligibility and, I would soon see, ventriloquistic legibility as well.

Penguin, that is, played as though possessed, Drennette as though feeding him his lines. He was her put-upon amanuensis. She was prompter and psychopomp both. He spoke thru the horn as though telling of a dream while still asleep, a waking dream whose theme was dreamt conveyance. Behind the lids of my closed eyes I saw the words he spoke inscribed within the blank he had previously drawn, written out and rolling within the template, rolling scroll and teleprompter into one, ancient and modern into one. *In my head I composed a letter I knew by heart* were the first words to appear.

Drennette's inventiveness made the drums a laboratory of sorts. Penguin rolled actor and lab technician into one, rendering his lines with the attentiveness to detail of a lab report. Drennette's "findings" were anything but clinical, however. She goaded and cursed with a slurred insinuation and a possessed insistence worthy of Elvin's work with Trane. Compelled by and competing with dream, resentful of dream, she thumped out a spate of disconsolate patter on the bass drum. No less compelled by and competing with dream and resentful of dream, but also compelled by and competing with drum and resentful of drum, Penguin soliloquized as if to negotiate between grist and beguilement, ghost and beguilement, rival memory and dreamt revival, dream and drum. Admittedly beholden to Drennette's drum-lab chatter, he had much that was his own to say as well.

As Penguin's bari spoke, the words continued to appear within the template, written out on the teleprompted scroll the music unfurled: *But, no, I was not Djeannine, I only dreamt I was. . . .* It occurred to me that the template amounted to something of a balloon. Given the script's overt reference to balloons, it was clear that what was going on was a B'Loon visit. B'Loon was granting what had become our not so secret wish that the balloons appear, if at all, in a more subtle, less attention-getting way. This latest visit thus took an esoteric turn, removing the words from open view, advancing a script only the closed eye saw. B'Loon had gone underground I understood. We had survived our brief encounter with fame.

B'Loon's presence was further confirmed by the wind which gradually arose from Drennette's drumset as Penguin soloed. As at Soulstice in Seattle, where the balloons made their first appearance, Drennette brewed a spinning wind with each roll she resorted to. Answering Penguin's rhythmic aplomb, the rhythm instrument the bari became, she made the drums a wind instrument, ventilated his grist with beguiling gusts. I felt a breeze at my back, especially so on the back of my neck.

Drennette's drum-driven wind gradually blew with more force as Penguin soloed, peaking, appropriately, just as he concluded, both it and the teleprompted script all the more forcefully announcing B'Loon's presence: *My high notes harbored B'Loon's beakful of mud*.

When Penguin ended his solo I opened my eyes and put my horn to my mouth. He, Lambert and I embarked on the next unison passage, following which Aunt Nancy soloed, as planned. Following Aunt Nancy's solo, we repeated the long, labyrinthine unison passage my solo normally follows. This we did to allow me the solo space Penguin preempted, having whispered among ourselves to that effect while Aunt Nancy soloed. I took my solo, after which we returned to the head and ended the piece. We played one more number, "The Slave's Day Off," whereupon we got called back for an encore and offered a short, sololess reading of "Half-Staff Appetition."

As usual, a few friends and fans came backstage afterwards. We were curious, of course, as to whether any of them had closed their eyes during Penguin's solo and whether, if they had, they'd seen what I saw. It turned out that a couple of them had closed their eyes and they reported that indeed they had seen the teleprompted script. I spoke with both of them at length, comparing notes, as it were, taking notes. The words the three of us had seen, it became clear, were the same.

The only question now is what was it Aunt Nancy whispered in Penguin's ear. She won't say and neither will he. He says the one thing he will say is that she told him not to.

Yours,

N.

Dear Angel of Dust,

Today at rehearsal Lambert told us about a dream he had
last night. He was in the backyard, he says, to a house he
heard a voice coming out of, his mother's voice. He stood
before a patch of flowers, the house to his left, not looking
toward the house, caught up instead in the flowers in front of
him, oddly colored flowers—blue lilies, purple tulips, the
hues, moreover, metallic. He stood entranced, he says, by the
unusual sheen of the flowers' petals, the various grades of
metallic blue or metallic purple on a given petal, burnt bur-
nish to mirrorlike bright. He heard his mother's voice coming
out of the house and it seemed he heard it from closer to the
house than he actually was, though he wasn't looking at the
house, he says, and thus can't say how he knew what the dis-
tance was. It seemed he partook of two lookings, he says. He
looked at the flowers and he also had eyes on the back of his
head—not eyes *at* the back of his head, he insists, eyes *on* it.
He seemed to be subject to as well as wielding a stare which
looked at him from behind, saw him in relation to the house
without him looking at the house.

Lambert says he heard his mother, who's been dead five
years, talking inside the house, talking in a tone of voice that
she used to use with him when he was a child. He knew he
was in some unusual realm even as he dreamt, he says, the
land of the dead perhaps, that of dream at the very least, pos-
sibly both (dream, it crossed his mind even as he dreamt,
could play psychopomp). He listened more and more intently,
hungrily, happy and sad to again hear that voice—happy to be
hearing it at all, sad that it could be heard only there in this
unusual realm. He continued looking at the blues and purples

of the lilacs and tulips' petals, looking at the flowers but listening to his mother's voice, listening more intently than looking. So intent was his listening, he says, it seemed he could see her inside the house talking to him as a little boy, see himself as a little boy inside the house. Though it seemed he could see inside the house without looking, he was so happy to hear his mother's voice and so hungry to see more he turned and looked toward the house, at which point the house disappeared, taking her voice with it.

Lambert calls the dream an "Orphic warning." He said it speaks to what he termed "our current situation," that he saw no need to elaborate, that he wouldn't say more.

He didn't need to. We all, without discussing it, saw what he meant.

Yours,
N.

house. What Penguin sought to prove thru the press of lips, a perhaps redundant press of lips it turns out, proves in crucial ways to be the far side of carnal capture, far beyond empirical presence or proof. What he sought to prove (more to himself than to anyone else it would seem) was what he's been saying all along, that there's more to Drennette than meets the eye. But that this could be true of the lip as well as the eye has some bearing I'm not yet altogether clear about on the default on captionless being to which the balloons attest. The advent of intervening sleep at the very moment their lips were poised to meet has something to do with renouncing redundant proof, incongruous proof, with positing a Monk-like renunciative harmonic which, albeit warm with the rub of empirical pressure, remains wise to fallacious equations of pressure with proof. It proposes, instead, an aliquant equation of verge-of-a-kiss with virgin kiss, virgin kiss with virgin cognition. Penguin's intervening sleep adduced an incumbent press of limbs and lips, virgin kiss qua cognizance, alternate embrace, vatic, ostensible embrace as if of nothing and if of nothing only of nothing-to-prove. Duke said something that's relevant here, not once and for all but to be revisited again and again: "Prelude to a Kiss." Penguin's intervening sleep took the accent off of proof and put it on prelude, drawing, as his Aunt Nancy-prompted solo also would, on unmarked as well as marked ambiguations of sexual and sacred, sophic and sacrilegious, secular and sacred, body and soul.

Lambert oscillates between saying it was bound to happen, that Drennette and Penguin were bound to, as he puts it, "get it on dreamwise," and doubting that what Aunt Nancy told Penguin is true, dismissing her talk of Drennette having dreamt the Djeannine dream as a motivating fiction, a lie she told to get Penguin to play. I myself have no doubts. Drennette dreaming the Djeannine dream says to me that

Penguin's "ass eye" saw more than it saw, that the see-thru
amenities glass affords leaves one nonetheless blind to fraught
furtherances of sight, synaesthetic impactednesses only a tac-
tile eye could apprehend. Drennette's "caressive receptivity"
and corresponding "ass eye" crossed an otherwise unbridge-
able divide to barter broken-tooth resolve with ain'thropologic
distraint. The *feel* of Kashmiri Cough Drops in Penguin's
mouth took hold of her mouth, a circumlocutious kiss whose
virgin precincts ("the hill with the sun behind her," "the
meadow at the foot of the hill") boasted waters glass-bottom
boats patrol. Derived from a soft-focus, near-homophonous
equation of booth with boat, such vessels advanced a dreamt
occlusion whereby see-thru bottom concerted glass with ass.
Penguin picked up on this in his Aunt Nancy-prompted solo:
"Mud brought all the way from the Nile. . . ." Mud from Lake
Dal it could just as easily have been. In any case, to so elevate
mud signals having grown wise to see-thru pretense.

Glass occlusion, after all, isn't all that far-fetched. I still
remember looking at a drop of water under a microscope for
the first time in a science class in grammar school. The osten-
sibly clear water could be seen to be teeming with microor-
ganisms, crowded with tiny forms of life made visible only by
arrangements of glass. The lens allowed one to see thru clarity
itself, see thru to complicating, occluding forms and features
one would otherwise not have seen. Glass put mud in one's
eye. Ostensible sheerness's occultation was a glass-enhanced
recognition of apparent stillness as recondite motility, appar-
ent stasis as unseen agitation, an endlessly adaptive dance.

The latter phrase is Julius Hemphill's. He says that "A.D."
in the title of his piece "Dogon A.D." stands for Adaptive
Dance, that it came out of his reading an article about the
Dogon deciding to reveal some of their sacred dance rituals
to attract the tourist trade. Before hearing this I took it to

mean Anno Domini, as most people probably do. The appropriateness of this to an adaptive accord between purity and commerce, compromise, makes each meaning fit, work in more than one way. Penguin and Drennette's dream exchange, virgin kiss though it was, adaptively sustained a default on supposed purity, a default (aka mud) whose compromise with commerce (bought kisses, slot-machine eyes) adumbrated an array of subtle adjustments, a sublime, all but microbic pas de deux.

However personal its reach and whatever its roots, Penguin's Aunt Nancy-prompted solo also aired anxieties we've been feeling about the balloons and, more obliquely, the visibility we can't help hoping to gain by cutting a record. Penguin again proved to be our plumb line. Perhaps it bodes well for our upcoming record date that the spectre of cartoon accessibility could itself, like Bird's Woody Woodpecker quotes, be drawn into the music.

So, yes, it's graduation time, time for us to either put aside our forebodings or consume them, feed ourselves, learn how to use them as fuel. It's time to go forward—with a lag-leg stride if need be, but go forward—burn with a variously adaptive dance and adieu, begin to bid apprehension goodbye. Drennette's tripping over a strand of phantom kelp, freighted, we now see, with the weight of having dreamt the Djeannine dream, may well have been a step in the right direction.

A part of me thinks we should quote "Pomp and Circumstance" at some point in the album, play upon Penguin and Drennette's dreamt, soft-focus coupling of commerce and commencement, a double-aspected walk-down-the-aisle. But that would be going too far.

As ever,

N.

12.IX.82

Dear Angel of Dust,

Thank you for your letter. Yes, you read me right. Drennette stumbling over a phantom strand of kelp, going down, albeit briefly, on all fours to bounce right back up, was an adaptive step in a staggered ballet of which Penguin's "Wind-Assisted Drum-Lab Readout" and she and Penguin dreaming reciprocal dreams were respectively later and earlier steps. Her accidental prostration, moreover, flirts with an evocation of reminiscent entwinement as implicitly prayerful, intimations of limbed entanglement rolling animal and religious fidelities into one. Her and Penguin's courtship, if that's what it is, is an adaptive dance drawn out over disparate points in time, cloistered and courtly both, an eight-limbed enablement proposing retreat as a kind of advance, virtual or virgin clasp as immaterially bound beyond empirical demise. So as to touch without touching, each abdicated his or her dream in the his-and-her dreamhouse, a devotional default which granted them both translative passage between horn and drum, ventriloquial pitch apportioning immaculacy and mud. So, at any rate, it seems to me.

We played at a place in Long Beach called the Blue Light Lounge last night. It was a gig which had its moments, the one that stays with me most being one that occurred as we were playing "Altered Cross." Lambert was soloing on tenor, Aunt Nancy behind him on bass, Djamilaa on piano, Drennette on drums. He was into a deep crouch, bent over, his horn all but grazing the floor, bellowing as though caught in some harsh quandary, as though "altered" were a fractious play on "altared," conflicted claims mixing sanctity and sacrilege. He thrashed and brayed, a voice from the depths, but suddenly Aunt Nancy, Djamilaa and Drennette broke into an uptempo bossa nova, a bounding, waltz-time extenuation for which Drennette's stick on the snare's metal rim kept time with even measures of mirth and residual menace, ambidextrous foil and fellow traveller to Djamilaa's light but elated right hand. Aunt Nancy's bass figure evinced a tidelike ebb and flow, a lusty, recurrent swell and subsidence, the four fingers of her left hand scurrying about the bass's fingerboard like an alarmed half-spider. The bass line, it seemed, said it all, though in this instance "all" meant no saying said enough.

Lambert, taken by surprise, relied at first on a captious, expectorant croon reminiscent of Shepp's way of playing "The Girl from Ipanema," a now abrasive, now caressive growl with which he bought time. However, time bought, new bearings gotten, he took a mellower tack, a forthright ride of the rhythm section's roll and recurrence, a willingness to be carried along, even carried away, a transparent, it-doesn't-bother-me facade by way of which he backed away from his earlier abject air. Punctuating such willingness and the wave it rode, however, was an intermittent pass in which Lambert, meditative, sotto voce, let the rhythm section chime louder behind him. It was a turning to himself which bespoke misgiving, albeit misgiving mixed with guileful resolve. It seemed he reasoned with a troublesome remnant of his earlier disarray, pestered but philosophic, up to the task. It was a good example of what John Gilmore means by "contrary motion." The rhythm section's bodily blare and relentless forwarding were countered by Lambert's reflective step back, such misgiven retreat a clearly fictive sublation whose insinuative trace proffered ghost and body both.

Neither hoarse nor laryngitic, Lambert's sotto voce tack resonated, a soliloquistic aside whose elegiac reflection on the furtherance the rhythm section fostered freighted such furtherance with a bittersweet adamance, as though time were so infectiously marked only to lament its loss. But Drennette, head held high, resolutely tapping the rim of the snare, would have none of this—or would have it, having to, only in such mixed-emotional array as Djamilaa's bright right-hand proclamations and Aunt Nancy's ambulant ebb and flow brewed or brought out. Time slipped away, she allowed, but only to be swung by the track or trail it drew with it. It was frighteningly beautiful the way they brokered so duplicit a peace with the passing of time.

Getting back to your letter: no, we haven't worked out which pieces we'll put on the album. Our book's gotten so big we may have to make it a two-record set to keep the omissions to a minimum. We'd like to include a piece or two not written by one of us, "Sun Ship," say, or "Like A Blessed Baby Lamb," but that makes the question of which of our own to include tougher. Probably what we'll do is spend all day in the studio, record everything in our book and then decide which ones came out best. Anyway, we'll see. You're still interested in writing the liner notes we hope.

Yours,
N.

PS: No sign of the balloons at last night's gig.

25.IX.82

Dear Angel of Dust,

The recording session went well, much more smoothly than we'd expected. Aside from the minor, inevitable hitch here and there, none of our nervousness and apprehension seems to have been justified. In fact, it may be that our nervousness and apprehension got big enough to be an unexpected boon, a roundabout blessing. It's tempting, at least, to see it that way. We got to where we were rehearsing everyday, some days almost all day, so intent were we on getting everything down, on everything going according to plan, on there being a plan. So impressed were we by the thought of the music being immortalized in wax we wanted to make it perfect, provide for all contingencies, leave as little as possible to chance. The recording session loomed so large, came to be so fraught with ultimacy, we mistakenly wanted it all worked out in advance. The closer we got to the recording date the more obsessed we got. It was Drennette who, in her roundabout way, finally straightened us out.

Four days, that is, before the day we recorded we had a rehearsal we had to call off because of Drennette not showing up. As it turned out, she was nowhere to be found up until the very day we recorded, showing up at the studio, drumset in tow, ready to play, much to our relief though not entirely to our surprise. Not long after the aborted rehearsal, that very same day in fact, Aunt Nancy, Djamilaa, Lambert, Penguin and I had all found the same "message" on our answering machines. Someone had called each of us and played a line from a song on the *Black Orpheus* soundtrack album into the receiver, recorded the same line from the same song on all our machines. The song was "A Felicidade," the line "e cai como uma lágrima." Whoever it was had made a loop of it, letting it repeat exactly seven times before hanging up, giving it the sound of a needle stuck on a nicked record.

Once we put it together that this was the case, that we'd all gotten the same "message" at what must've been about the same time, and put this together with Drennette, within roughly the same span of time, not having shown up for rehearsal and now being nowhere to be found, we suspected the coincidence was no coincidence, that the *Black Orpheus* "message" and Drennette's disappearance were connected. It took hardly any discussion at all to conclude that Drennette had left the "message" on our machines, that, taking a page out of Penguin's book (or, earlier, Lambert's), she had gone into retreat, a preparatory retreat, a retreat the "message" announced while leaving us food for thought. Drennette, we surmised, had gone off "to prepare a place," a place, premise or permission from which to better leverage our recording venture, leaving the rest of us to reflect on the "message" she'd left on our answering machines.

The line means "and falls like a tear." Was this Drennette's way of admitting that she had fallen, not leapt, the day she and Djamilaa walked along the shore at Santa Monica Beach? Was she now allowing there'd been no phantom strand of kelp over which to trip, only pathos, her own choked-up emotion, that she'd in fact fallen "like a tear"? Was she suggesting, confessing, obliquely but even so, that *leapt* was less what her plummet was tantamount to, amounted to, than *wept*? It surely appeared so, though what we soon enough saw was that the more important, more instructive message for us was that she'd found a way to say this without saying it. Roundabout to the bone, she was saying, we soon enough saw, not so much something about what happened at the beach as about us. Say it without saying it she seemed to insist, yet there was more.

Didn't the needle-stuck-on-a-nick accent senses of impairment, imperfection, a recognition she meant to bring us back to in the face of our wished-for immaculacy? That she "spoke" with nicked-record insistence, played upon the wear, the maculation endemic to the premises we extolled, would-be states of recorded grace our obsessed rehearsals prepared for, pursued, by no means escaped our notice.

The decisive thing, though, was that with Drennette gone we couldn't go on rehearsing. This ultimately worked to the recording date's advantage, forcing us to loosen up, to let go of our wish to work everything out in advance. Drennette had taken it upon herself to bring our obsessed rehearsals to an end, get us to relax, going into retreat as if to say to us, "Lighten up. Cool it." This occurred to us readily enough once we saw that she was nowhere to be found. Nudging our thoughts in this direction was the recording on her answering machine. When we called her apartment, that is, we found that she'd replaced her spoken greeting with the recording of Trane's voice on the *Sun Ship* album, the comments he makes to the other musicians right before "Dearly Beloved": "Keep, keep, you know, keep a *thing* happening all thru it." This hit us as being directed our way, meant to say something specifically to us, the permissive indefiniteness of Trane's inclusive "*thing*" pointedly contrasting with our recent, exaggerated wish for definitiveness.

Still, all of this was inferred, shadowed by the risk of being wrong inference runs. We could be wrong we knew. We could be totally misreading the situation. We couldn't be certain that Drennette hadn't simply gotten fed up with us, that she hadn't broken down (fallen like a tear), unable to function, that things weren't amiss in some other way. We had no way of being sure that all of this had been orchestrated by her as we hoped and suspected, that on the day of the recording she'd show up.

Though we were confident, all but certain, even, we'd have said, convinced, we nonetheless knew we could be wrong. Thus it was that when Drennette did show up on the day of the recording we were relieved, albeit not surprised.

It went farther than simple relief though. That we'd read Drennette right, that she'd successfully "said it without saying it," not only taught by example but advanced an angular rapport we felt buoyed up by, buoyed up and newly borne along by. It further loosened us up, helped us lighten up, confirmed a certain chemistry we thereby took into the studio with us, an oblique articulacy's jointure and drape, indirect address. Aunt Nancy later resorted to a basketball metaphor to describe it: "It was as though she threw us a no-look pass." Albeit implicitly disavowed, Drennette's phantom strand of kelp informed us throughout, an exposed nerve or its referred sensation, so persistent a report we needed only abide by the auspice it proffered. Indeed, no-look obliquity blessed us with a prescient, post-optic aptitude in Orphic disguise, Orphic bind borne as roundabout reprieve. Hence the title we've decided on for the album, *Orphic Bend*.

I could say more about the music and the recording session itself, but I won't beyond enclosing a new after-the-fact lecture/libretto, a new installment I found myself writing these past couple of days. Impelled in large part by aliquant reminders of the session's look-without-looking aplomb, its no-look élan, the lecture/libretto may prove of some use as you go about writing your liner notes. Also enclosed are tapes of the music, all of what we recorded. We've no more than begun deciding which pieces and which takes will go on the album. As always, we welcome your thoughts.

Yours,

N.

DOOR PEEP
(SHALL NOT ENTER)

or, The Creaking of the Word: After-the-Fact
Lecture/Libretto (Djband Virgin)

The fall of Hotel Didjeridoo reverberated worldwide. In Southern California a wave washed a bottle ashore, a note-bearing bottle, the bottle B'Loon had finally been put into, put back into. Cat-out-of-the-bag, horse-out-of-the-barn and genie-out-of-the-lamp rolled into one, B'Loon, while out of the bottle, had written the note the bottle now bore, a note apprising the world of its whorehouse roots. Dubbed "Namesake Encyclical #1," it was a simple note. Referring to the brothels in which "jazz" was reportedly born, the words it bore were these: "And the girls would come down dressed in the finest evening gowns, just like they were going to the opera." Hotel Didjeridoo, it meant to announce, had been such a house.

The word from down under was thus that the music guests had heard piped into their rooms was overdetermined inversion, a music making fun of its mock-operatic roots, opera making fun of its presumed elevation. That such elevation had a hand in its own undoing was thought by many to have helped bring Hotel Didjeridoo down. The girls, everyone knew, put on their evening gowns only to take them off. To do so they went back up. This was the opera they ascended to.

So, at least, the analysis went. Djbouche, however, had tired of such analysis. The note, he knew, existed at his expense. B'Loon had agreed to go back into the bottle only on the condition that the note go in with him, that room be made for the note by evicting Djbouche, his longtime bottle-mate (drinking buddy, according to some). Thus it was that Djbouche too blew into town, washed ashore in an alternate bottle, a noteless bottle, bent on teaming up again with B'Loon, performing a duet. That "jazz" played low note to opera's high note, he insisted, everybody already knew. What he wanted was to play no note to B'Loon's low note. Thus the noteless bottle he blew into town in.

Still, Djbouche was no angel. It was he who had exposed the goings-on at Hotel Didjeridoo, he who had played Peeping Tom raconteur one time too many, he who had tended the Keyhole Club Convention's no-host bar. Though his "No-Note Samba" had more than fit the occasion, he felt depleted, deprived, deserving of greater recognition, wanting, however much he knew better, to be the commercial lubricant his no-note tack took issue with. It was, after all, he who had put the bug in B'Loon's ear, he who had whispered, "Give them what they want."

What the ubiquitous, indefinite "they" wanted was to see, to be able to say what they saw was what they got. This is what B'Loon had delivered. To dress for the opera was to be at the opera. To undress was to bring opera down. It all but went without saying they'd get no more than what they saw, all but amounted to insisting they could see getting only what they saw. "Show them a good time," Djbouche had whispered in B'Loon's ear.

Djbouche, claiming to be no angel but no Mephistopheles either, now blamed the bug he'd put in B'Loon's ear on the heady spirits he'd had the job of serving at the Keyhole Club Convention's no-host bar. "The fumes must've gotten to me," he told himself, more and more convinced that the mere smell of alcohol had loosened his tongue, caused him to speak too freely. Speakeasy premises, he told himself, had taken hold of him, caused him to speak on behalf of slurred speech, slurred but articulate seen-said merger, seen-said auction-block lubricity fusing lucidity with bottom-line sex.

The effect of the fumes confirmed the power of scent over sound, sound over sight. What the ubiquitous, indefinite "they" saw had been dictated by what B'Loon had to say, what B'Loon had to say by the heady whiff Djbouche couldn't help catching while tending bar. The greater recognition Djbouche was intent on gaining for the alternate bottle in which he washed ashore would in part be gained by the theory he came prepared to advocate. It was a theory which would supplant B'Loon's founding script or founding scratch with a notional/anti-notational elision. Founding nose would elide founding noise as what preceded so-called founding script, *founding nose* anti-notationally rendered *founding no(i)se*. The parenthetic *i* would signify an imaginary operation whereby scent pervaded sound, sound scent.

The complex, multifaceted phenomena known collectively as Hotel Didjeridoo, Djbouche came ready to argue, rested on a submerged, fleetingly recognized bottom line, synaesthetic sniff. Hotel Didjeridoo had gone down like Atlantis, a utopic union of sound and scent whose prelapsarian allure held optic ascendancy in check—a plummet or plunge whose latest report would be the newly arrived "Theory of Founding No(i)se" itself. Founding no(i)se, to which B'Loon's mud was related as table to indentation, had been known in an earlier report as "Funk Underneath." Djbouche, with namesake propriety, would lend no(i)se a Franco-Maghrebi inflection, relating it to the bottle in which he washed ashore by posing between-the-sheets musk as winelike fragrance, *djboudoir-djbouteille-djbouquet* as the chord he'd have struck had the bottle not been noteless, a theoretico-subjunctive chord to which an alternate Namesake Encyclical would attach.

For years Miles Davis had been saying of bebop: "We were like scientists of sound. If a door squeaked we could call out the exact pitch." Had Djbouche's bottle borne a note, a

Namesake Encyclical, the words written on it would have been those. However much he insisted on between-the-sheets bouquet, Djbouche wanted most to ally brain with bottom-line sex. "Hotel Didjeridoo had a bar but no lab," he was fond of saying. "That's why it went down." The new edifice his duet with B'Loon would erect would roll bottle and beaker into one, sonance and science (chemical wedding) into one.

B'Loon, however, had bigger plans. The duet, as far as he was concerned, had already begun. The point was to parlay it into a stint with Djband, an up-and-coming combo he had long admired and on a few occasions even sat in with. Eligible advent was the name he'd given it, the sitting in, but he'd have been the first to say he'd made a mistake, legible advent—the first, had Djbouche not beaten him to it. This was the sense in which the duet had already begun. Djbouche chided him for misread eligibility, legible snafu, an antiphonal rejoinder B'Loon didn't hear so much as feel, nonsonant demur. It was as much duel as duet, a bout between contending ways of being.

Though he'd have been the first to say he'd made a mistake, B'Loon blamed it on his childhood, the Farmer Alfalfa cartoons he'd watched as a child. Backed, as they were, by Ellington's music, they'd made an ineradicable impression it seemed, equating the music with cartoon clarity, an impression which had come back to haunt him as legible advent, presumed hyperintelligibility, pictographic imprint, scripted sense.

The balloon-borne legibility B'Loon had adduced from Djband's music bespoke a misconceived cartoon limpidity he could hardly believe he'd ever imagined, much less introduced on those occasions on which, uninvited by Djband, he'd sat in. Though the term *caption*, strictly speaking, didn't apply to what he'd done, he nonetheless thought of it in that regard, chiding himself for the suggestion of *capture* he couldn't help hearing, the presumed abatement of sound's prodigal behest.

Such misgiving had paved the way for B'Loon agreeing to be put back in the bottle. Self-chiding proved to be the beginning of dialogue, the root of duet. B'Loon's qualms were Djbouche's eligible advent, the foot-in-the-door he awaited, unaware it was already there.

Still, however much self-doubt seeded the duet, the fact was that Djbouche's critique of speakeasy fluidity applied to cartoon limpidity as well. It could not have remained lost for long on either him or B'Loon that the music's presumed whorehouse roots were related to presumptions of cartoon clarity, that bottom-line sex exchanged clarity of aegis and intent for what was otherwise fraught with ambiguity, innuendo, traded redeemed, "operatic" mud for aporetic mud. Born-again mud made common coin of sex, sold it for what it thereby became, explain-all base. Love of sex, everyone knew, was the root of such music. Thus it was that in a well-known cartoon Betty Boop ran with Louis Armstrong in hot pursuit. It was a cartoon B'Loon and Djbouche had both seen as kids.

Aporetic mud nonetheless persisted. Explain-all sex undermined its own foundation, aroused expectations it couldn't fulfill. The bottom it sought to secure slid, shifted, wouldn't stay put. Bottom-line lubricity proved a weak antidote to slippage. All of this B'Loon and Djbouche had on good authority. Drennette Scientist had long ago noted that sex too boasted a prodigal behest. This B'Loon and Djbouche both knew, though neither knew that the other knew, she having spoken to each apart from the other.

Drennette Scientist (also known as Drennette Virgin) had made each of them feel it was more a test tube than a bottle he was in. She advocated carrying funk back to Ki-Kongo *lu-*

fuki, a transitive accord between scent and science, root sense of integrity, sweat invested in the working out of the art. This she did to countervail against reductions of funk to a play for commercial appeal, bottom-line sweat as commercial lubricant, bass-line whiff the market's muscular bouquet (auction-block bouquet). She spoke of "Hard Work," John Handy's big hit, saying that its love of labor was to be endorsed but that there needed to be a concurrent, epistatic unsettling of bottom-line barter, bedrock swap. She spoke on behalf of what she termed "laboratory sweat," an anti-anti-sublime titration aimed at funk no longer precluding perfume.

Perfume, it had struck both B'Loon and Djbouche, was an odd, unessential item for Drennette Virgin to be endorsing, but in light of its synthetic aspect and her Drennette Scientist aspect it all made perfect sense. She sought, they'd come separately to understand, a sublime, no longer sublimated accord between ascetic and synthetic, a concomitant accord between synthetic and synaesthetic, epistatic funk and pheromonal sway.

Such admonitions regarding bedrock swap helped Djbouche prevail against the feeling of being deprived, his intermittent wish for greater recognition, the sort of lapse into commercial aspiration which had led him to tell B'Loon, "Give them what they want." His "No-Note Samba" sought to further the sense of epistatic funk Drennette Scientist had adumbrated. He was her test tube, willingly so, happily so. Samba's characteristic bass-drum thump, under his care, was displaced into what could be called splay disposition, backbeat as vagrancy (vacancy at points), no pat recurrence caroling pulse, pertinence, provision. Djbouche's no-note tack accented nonsonant "bump," a noncorpuscular virtuality whose quantum élan had driven the Keyhole Club Conventioneers wild. What they "heard" (more thought they heard

than heard, felt more than thought) was temporality partaken
of, made palpable, time's passage saluted and lamented all at
once, as though "bump" were a protuberant breach they
bought into, bought and bid goodbye in the same breath.
Epistasis notwithstanding, pulse, a certain tolling insistence,
was very much alive in what Djbouche proposed. How he
managed to avail himself of samba's amenities while dispens-
ing with its usual trappings was the cause of many a head
being scratched.

How Djbouche was able to tend bar and perform at the
same time caused many a head to be scratched as well, so
cathartic was the nonsonant "bump" he filled the air with.
Indeed, it was feeling more than anything else, a felt filling-
up of the air with an unspecified something one sensed would
not otherwise have been there. The Keyhole Club
Convention had been the last major event to take place at
Hotel Didjeridoo before its collapse, a fact which led some to
believe Djbouche's felt-fill "bump" had had something to do
with its fall, the same unspecified something one had felt fill
the air throughout the bar, lobby and lounge. The ascetic-sci-
entific spin Djbouche had visited upon samba, they averred,
had had unforeseen, cataclysmic repercussions. It was as if,
they ventured further, nonsonant "bump" were to samba what
black holes were to stars, a pit of antithetic density and con-
centration all approach to which proffered collapse as
ineluctable egress, bottom-line "get."

Part of Djbouche's job as bartender was to chat with cus-
tomers, lend a friendly ear and offer entertaining talk. The
latter he'd given particular attention during the Keyhole Club
Convention, regaling conventioneers at the no-host bar with
graphic tales of goings-on upstairs, peepshow accounts of the
"operatic" doings in various rooms. What he offered was
namesake perspective (keyhole perspective) on the bottom-

line sex taking place above their heads. This and the nonsonant "bump" of his "No-Note Samba," to say nothing of the drinks he served, provided a one-two punch which had many a conventioneer reeling—reeling, yet coming back for more.

B'Loon had been surprised when Djbouche told him, "Give them what they want. Show them a good time." He had been even more surprised when, on his way out of the hotel, he'd come upon Djbouche entertaining conventioneers at the no-host bar. The moment they made eye contact he saw a twinge of embarrassment shoot across Djbouche's face. It reminded him of the story Benny Golson tells of happening upon Trane honking atop a bar in a club in Philadelphia one night and of Trane's embarrassment and the sheepish grin he wore afterwards, having once told Golson he'd never stoop to "walking the bar." Djbouche, however, wore no sheepish grin. He fought his embarrassment back with bravado, motioning B'Loon over to the bar and answering the question he took it B'Loon wanted to ask but wouldn't (or, if he would, beating him to the punch), whispering in his ear as if resigned to a new, disillusioning truth, "Give them what they want. Show them a good time."

B'Loon had not been unaware of bravado's role in what Djbouche whispered, but the statement had surprised him nonetheless. Even more surprising had been the extent to which it hit home, the extent to which B'Loon took it seriously, heard it as an indictment, a snide condemnation of legible advent, the cartoon-clear, literalizing spirit he'd become on those occasions he sat in with Djband.

B'Loon had in fact been on his way out of the hotel that night to sit in with Djband again. The bug Djbouche put in his ear, the snide exhortation to sell out which he heard as accusing him of having sold out, led him to take a more subtle tack. Yes, he reflected guiltily, the legibility he lent the music not only sold it out but sold it short, relieved its listeners of the brunt of incommensurability it meant them to bear, the prodigal stir it wanted them to abide by, digest. Yes, he admitted, the balloon-borne wordage he'd adduced from the music could be taken the wrong way—not as food for thought but as immediatist instinct, something which obviated thought. Yes, he admitted, it had maybe been naive to hope otherwise, fanciful to think he could prevail against cognitive shortcut, notions of an instinctualist language, an instinctualist people's default on language. Yes, there was a long history of exactly that shortcut, a history not to be easily dismissed or too soon forgotten, easy attributions regarding "a tropical race who typify the life of feeling, deficient in the power of abstract thought." It was disconcerting to find himself possibly perpetuating such attribution, unwittingly complicit with grunt clarity, cartoon articulacy, captive address.

Such qualms had led B'Loon to agree to being put back in the bottle. Like Djbouche, he thought of it more as a test tube than a bottle, happily gave Drennette Scientist his support, hoping by that to undo whatever damage he might have done. The prospects implied by virgin science appealed to him immensely. His, he thought, was a dream (even if only a dream) which befit Djband's imminent trek into the recording studio, an erotic-elegiac wish to revisit firstness, know first knowing again. The contradiction didn't escape him, which is in part what gave the wish its elegiac rub, made it the outcome of sad science perhaps, nescience no. His wish took advantage of the imminent trek being Djband's first, a fact he sought to parlay, should the stint he had in mind materialize, into more than incidental fact, more than mere contingency, more than a bleak choice between metaphor and metonym, more than Djband would otherwise know, firstness notwithstanding.

Perhaps Djband itself was a vain dream of union B'Loon sometimes thought, belated quest for first knowledge, first-known fullness, founding cement. There were those who contended science was inevitably sad, that Hotel Didjeridoo, severed sensation's last resort, had been bound to fall, that this was the crash whose everlasting report sad science rehearsed. Drennette Scientist, however, in a letter to B'Loon dated "Any day now," advocated a virgin science, augured its advent, insisted on sound as a recombinant medium pinning virgin hope on aporetic mud. The thought of this letter, which had arrived a few days before the fall of Hotel Didjeridoo, bolstered B'Loon's hope of teaming up with Djbouche and of him and Djbouche teaming up with Djband.

Djbouche's no-note samba's nonsonant "bump" brushed against him again, a compression effect like a sonic boom without the boom. He felt it fill the bottle in which he washed ashore in much the way it had filled the bar, lounge and lobby as he was on his way out of Hotel Didjeridoo. The recurrent "bump" seemed likewise to augur a new science, ictic non-sound a cardiognostic virginity of address, as though to be so brushed was to know and be known for the very first time. How such virginity renewed itself had somehow to do with aporetic mud's precipitance, the "how" and the "somehow" the very crux of mud, what made it mud, the aporeticity of aporetic mud.

It was a mystery. "Bumped" recurrence lapped against the glass like water against the pilings of a pier. B'Loon let himself be rocked by it—boat, cradle, baby prophet among the rushes, whatever it took to bear the eviscerating buoyancy "bump" induced.

"Fond elixir," B'Loon muttered, more to himself than to the nonsonant "bump" he ostensibly addressed. Watery trope notwithstanding, "bumped" recurrence remained a dry run, a test run which, for all its undulance, left the liquidity it would eventually effect to some future date, "fond" imminence or impendence a felt-fill solution suffusing the air.

Again he muttered, "Fond elixir," awash with "bumped" recurrence's dry caress. Each arid "bump" wafted evaporative perfume, a nomadic, not-where-one-thought-it-would-be thump that rayed out, expanded, swelling toward a blow that never came or, if it did, dissolved, as its way of coming, into a ubiquitous, felt-fill rush. This was a further sense in which his and Djbouche's duet had already begun. The memory of non-sonant "bump" was no less with him than the note his bottle bore, a "fond" memento of his former bottle-mate and, he insisted, a harbinger of things to come.

Unseen but otherwise there, Drennette Scientist loomed larger than life, backdrop and animating breeze rolled into one, assisting the wave which washed the bottles ashore at Venice Beach, rechristened by the bottles' arrival, Venus Beach. Blown-bottle sonority filled the air, a hoarse but pen-etrant tone as of an Arabico-Berber flute. Faint, frail, it had the sound of having come a long way, the subtlest felt-fill sonority ever to have entered L.A. Very few of those at Venus Beach showed any sign of having heard it. The skaters went on skating as though nothing had happened, the weightlifters lifting weights as though nothing had hap-pened, tourists taking pictures as though nothing had hap-pened. All but a scattered few went on doing what they were doing as though nothing had happened. Those few, however, heard a frail, faint something endowing the otherwise ordi-nary sky with elegiac primer, sad-scientific base, virgin patina. Blown-bottle austerity attended by synthesizer strings made for a synthetico-symphonic sky, burgeoning crescendo endlessly all-but-absconded-with, beginning to bid sensation goodbye.

Those few turned their heads to see the source of what they heard but couldn't find it. Some of those who were sitting or who lay on their stomachs or backs stood up to get a better look, to no avail. What they saw was not the source of what they heard but one of its effects, an erotic-elegiac graininess bestowed upon or merely brought out in the surrounding flesh, tanning bodies on display, jogging bodies on display, weightlifting bodies on display, skating bodies on display. Blown-bottle sonority peppered all flesh with a flute-blown abrasion as of wind-blown sand, granted it a buff which was not untouched by weather, bruise, wear (grit-given scour, grit-given scratch).

Up to this point flesh had reclined lazily within itself, even that of those engaged in strenuous exertion. But with the advent of blown-bottle sonority a quality of strain, an aroused, ahead-of-itself nostalgia for bodily abidance, pervaded and could be seen on the skin of all those within view—seen with such acuity it seemed one could taste it. Sad-scientific foresight gave skin a spiked, philosophic savor, virgin science a newly provident salt, laboratory sweat.

Here and there the few who heard the blown-bottle sonority pinched or scratched or otherwise touched themselves, rubbed an arm or a leg or massaged a wrist, newly apprised of their bodies' unarrestable transit. The strung sky mourned an insistent furtherance it was also an exponent of, the risen power grit-given scratch had been taken to, "fond," empyrean scrub. The sound, faint and frail as it was, sharpened itself on skin and sky alike. Mimicking flesh or proposing a model for flesh, the sky too got a scoured look, wiped and rubbed with an abrasive agent which gave it a close-to-the-bone burnish (buffed ipseity, high-strung strop).

Faint, increasingly fraught, blown-bottle sonority kept close to the water and, once ashore, close to the ground. It

could well have been a broom, so sustained and adnate was
the sweep it advanced. It grazed the ocean and the shore with
an aspirate slide implying meek persistence, a readiness to
sweep them clean of water and sand, lose itself in the effort.
Such willingness to indulge futility compounded the press of
grainy transit imbued on the sky in the eyes of those who
heard it. Its futile willingness or wish to sweep sand and sea
away notwithstanding, it proposed itself as a potential coat, a
protective cover against vain endeavor.

It was an inoculative indulgence, it turned out, meant to
ward off undue expectation. This had to do with the ascetic-
scientific tack Djbouche, had his bottle borne a note, would
have expounded, been an exponent of. As it was, he found his
ostensibly no-note approach complicated by the sonic sweep
which bore him and B'Loon ashore. The blown-bottle sonor-
ity's willingness to indulge futility warned against a willingness
to woo frustration. It was nonetheless hard to know how to
read it, implicated as inextricably as he was. Indulgence as
antithetic omen bore a mixed message which further mixed
his own. This, he was beginning to find out, was what being in
a test tube meant.

Venus Beach, that is, had become an experimental site
presided over by Drennette Scientist on behalf of Djband, a
polyrhythmic lab conciliating erstwhile incongruences. She
sought a votive, talismanic solution which would bless
Djband's recording date, ward off commercial lubricancy's
lure without defaulting on juice.

Venus's in name only, Venus Beach was lab and altar both,
votive cabinet, an Afro-Atlantic "ultimate altar" brought to
the Pacific. Sea met sand as juice met drought, a borderline
vow that Djband's music become neither lubricious nor
unduly dry. Votive bottles leaned on test tube racks, around
which were test tubes half-immersed in sand. Set in cavities

dug deep in the sand to protect against wind were Bunsen burners lit to Iemandjá.°

Many more than the few who heard the blown-bottle sonority were those who had noticed Drennette Scientist's laboratory altar. It caught the eye of all who came near it, set in the sand not very far from the water's edge, an unusual sight even on a beach known for unusual sights. It was as though, for that small area at least, Venus Beach were a beach in Rio de Janeiro on New Year's Eve—an analogy neither lost on nor unintended by Drennette Scientist, who saw Djband's trek into the recording studio as a beginning, a new dawn or day or year which was not to be embarked on without asking for Iemandjá's blessing. A Brazilian would probably not have known what to make of the test tubes, test tube racks and Bunsen burners, but the green grapes, white roses and such would have been right at home at Ipanema or Copacabana— certainly moreso than at Venus Beach (where the test tubes, test tube racks and Bunsen burners were no less odd than they'd have been in Brazil).

Beachgoers happening past the laboratory altar walked over to it to get a better look. Some of them stooped or crouched or went down on one knee to take it in closer to ground level, poring over its various details and pondering the obvious attention to detail which had gone into it. Word had spread since the first sighting of the laboratory altar early that morning, so there were those who didn't simply happen upon

---

° Djeannine, Drennette Scientist's lab assistant/acolyte, insisted on spelling it with a "d" — this to further advance, by way of allusion, Drennette Scientist's theory of epistatic funk as well as pay respects to her own discographic roots. The cut which follows "Jeannine" on *Donald Byrd at the Half Note Cafe*, she never tired of pointing out, was "Pure D. Funk," the "d" in whose title, contrary to common use, was a mobile, epistatizing "d," one which got around. It had migrated to her name and done the same with Iemandjá.

it but came from elsewhere on the beach expressly to see it.
No one having seen Drennette Scientist and her lab assis-
tant/acolyte Djeannine as they worked on it well before dawn,
the question on many a lip was how had it gotten there, who
built it, why.

Many were those who had looked at the laboratory altar
and some of the few who heard the blown-bottle sonority
were among them. Very few were those who wondered was
there a connection between the two, but those who did were
on to more than they suspected. Had they gone so far as to
sniff or taste the liquid held by the test tubes, bowls and
beakers, the liquid they assumed to be seawater, they'd have
found it to be champagne. The significance of this they
wouldn't have gotten without also noticing that the sonority
had arisen as two bottles washed ashore, that the tide, flowing
farther up the beach than usual, had deposited the bottles at
the laboratory altar's very edge, in effect making them a part
of it. They would also have needed to notice that the bottles
were champagne bottles.

It was a very old story: bottle meets prow. Djband was a
boat the bottles were there to christen on this the day of its
maiden voyage, though they would not, as was custom, be
broken against its prow; the fall of Hotel Didjeridoo had
wrought breakage enough. Drennette Scientist, influenced
by her Drennette Virgin aspect, proffered a less literal meet-
ing, a sympathetic-parallactic alignment she nonetheless,
under the influence of Djeannine, likened to a kiss. Bottle,
she decided, would kiss prow from a distance, a dry, labora-
tory kiss with otherwise overt invocatory overtones—dry but
still a kiss, a dry kiss wet with the thought of champagne.

So it was that as B'Loon and Djbouche washed ashore
borne by champagne bottles at Venus Beach Djband was in a
recording studio on the other side of L.A. Arriving in separate

bottles made Djbouche's desire to team up with B'Loon all the more intense. Likewise, the bottles' long-distance address of Djband's prow kept B'Loon's desire to join Djband at peak strength. This was exactly what the Drennette Virgin aspect of Drennette Scientist had in mind, convinced that such impediment as distance purified desire, that such desire would be a boon to Djband, bless its maiden voyage.

Everything had fallen into place. Drennette Scientist/ Virgin, a tutelary projection based on one of Djband's members ("It's about cutting yourself in two," she'd been known to say), had taken it upon herself to both contain and garner the commitment of B'Loon and Djbouche, two exemplary souls who, intimate with bottom-line "get," could never be forgotten to be potential gremlins. They were there in the studio with Djband, though not literally so, parallactically present by way of a triangulated tryst whose two other points were Venus Beach and Hotel Didjeridoo. The mathematics had been worked out well in advance.

B'Loon and Djbouche were there in the studio with Djband from note one, beat one. They lent the music an urgency sifted free of undue anxiety, a weathered resilience free of resignation though not unwise to the uses of restraint. The recording engineer, after only a few bars, shook his head in astonishment, disbelief, not sure whether to trust or, if he did, what to make of what his ears reported.

There in the studio from the very first note of the very first take, B'Loon and Djbouche gave the riverine furtherance of Djband's first number a hint of hover, a haloing hint which mingled furtherance and float and which all who heard were at considerable pains to account for, unable to account for. The closest the recording engineer came was to say that it brought to mind and somehow managed to blend the world-weariness-resisting-itself of Ornette Coleman's "Antiques," the extended, oddly relaxed, extrapolative "alas" of Wayne Shorter's "De Pois do Amor, O Vazio" or Paulinho da Viola's "Cidade Submersa" and the plucked, ambulant ictus typical of Malinke music, the sort of thing he'd heard in certain pieces by Les Ambassadeurs du Mali or Les Amazones de Guinée.

B'Loon and Djbouche, there in the studio with Djband from the very moment the tape began to roll, gave riverine furtherance pause, an all but indetectable pause, made a certain peace with not knowing or with the limits of knowing, leaving the sound engineer to admit that it brought to mind and managed to blend all those things he'd named but that it didn't end there, that it blended all those things and more, that it did more than blend.

As did the recording engineer, others would hear that "more," all sides of it ("more" things, "more" than blending), the very "more" Djband's members rode like a boat, an adamant boat, glass-bottomed all the better to see the mud they rode above, borne aloft as though balloons lifted them up.